AVALON

QUEST FOR MAGIC

BOOK 1

Song of the Unicorns

by Rachel Roberts

AVALON
QUEST FOR MAGIC

BOOK 1

Song of the Unicorns

by Rachel Roberts

C·S Books

New York

First Edition

ISBN 1-59315-002-4

Cover Illustration by Jim Carroll
Cover Design by Richard Aquan

10 9 8 7 6 5 4 3 2

Prologue

The centaurs, half man, half horse, stood on a ledge overlooking a gorge. Long shadows fell across an ocean of mist. The bloodred sun dipped at their backs. Eliath, the first was called, shook the clinging damp from his hide and glanced north, then south.

The proud centaur lifted the silver amulet that hung from his neck. Beams of light shot from the object, casting a circular web of stars over the thick clouds that covered the open maw.

"I told you not to make that last jump," the other one, Corinth, complained. "We're not supposed to be here."

"I'd agree with you if I knew where 'here' was." Eliath studied the fairy map carefully, pinpoints of light reflecting in his wide, humanlike eyes.

One light blinked more brightly than the others. It meant that a portal lay a short distance ahead, but the only way to get there was to cross the gorge.

"There's another portal on the far side," Eliath observed.

"We can't trust the map," Corinth said, long tail swishing nervously. "The magic has been too unstable all along the web."

"You forget how important our mission is," Eliath said, nodding toward the wagon behind them. Inside the wagon, bursts of mournful wails like a wounded orchestra wafted over the lonely and desolate place.

"Are you sure the bridge is here?" Eliath asked.

Eliath altered the bubble of light, honing it to a sharp beam. It revealed a series of interconnected flat stones twisting their way across the gorge and then vanishing into the mist-shrouded far side.

"There," Corinth said, pointing. "The Demon's Crossing."

The wide stones floated precariously, moving and shifting to the silent rhythm of ancient magic.

"That bridge goes completely across?" Eliath asked.

Corinth stamped his forelegs to keep the icy chill from seeping up his thighs. Glancing to the covered wagon behind him, the centaur frowned. "We have no choice. We can't go back."

"Let's just move on," Eliath said sharply.

Corinth sighed and adjusted the shoulder

straps that hooked to long leather reins connecting to the large wagon.

The two centaurs moved carefully to the edge of the outcropping and stepped upon the floating bridge. It was solid as rock.

Mist curled over the stone like smoke as the wagon jostled forward. The centaurs could barely see their hooves.

"What was that?" Corinth shuddered, looking out across the bottomless chasm.

"There's nothing beneath us, all around us, but mist," Eliath answered. But something tingled across his shoulders, inched down his back—fear.

"I swear something is moving out there," Corinth insisted, craning his neck to look more closely into the swirling void.

Corinth was right. In the vast mass of clouds, something coalesced into a dark shape, moving—no—*swimming* through the mists.

"Let's move!" Eliath commanded.

But their steel horseshoes slipped on the damp rocks. The wagon staggered. A cacophony of screeches and whines rose from inside.

"Quiet!" Corinth hissed.

The centaurs moved quickly now, the wagon only narrowly avoiding the bridge's blunt edges and the perilous drop into nothing.

Suddenly, Corinth lurched backward, his hind

legs almost slipping over the edge. Eliath released the reins from his shoulder straps and trotted to the back of the wagon. The left rear wheel was wedged in a deep crevice that had been eaten away by centuries of icy wind.

The centaur lowered his shoulder and pushed against the wagon. Again, his cargo reacted with another chorus of angry and frightened sounds.

Muscles cording tight, Eliath strained. Sweat began to pour freely down his rich brown hide.

"Pull, Corinth!" Eliath yelled. "Harder!"

Then, a mass of something black flew across the wagon's path.

The wagon rolled forward.

Breathing hard, Eliath ran to the front of the wagon. He froze.

"Corinth?" He called out, looking left, then right. Torn reins fluttered in the wind. The other centaur had disappeared into the thick mist.

Snorting, Eliath tried to shake off the panic creeping into his chest. He quickly snapped the reins to his harness and pulled.

Black shapes swam all around now, skimming through the mists with terrifying speed. A sharp beam suddenly pierced the top of the wagon from within, sending splinters of wood flying. Jarring sounds screeched and squealed.

"No!" Eliath called over his shoulder. "You'll only make it worse!"

But it was too late. Like sharks to fresh blood, the mists roiled with huge black beasts. Too many! Eliath thought.

From the depths of the gorge, a razor fin sliced though the surface, coming right toward them.

With a mighty effort, Eliath pulled the wagon forward.

Bursts of light sent fireworks trailing as the wailing cries from the wagon turned to panicked screams.

Eliath tried to close his ears to the powerful forces building behind him. He swept the silver amulet from the chain around his neck, crisscrossing its light into a wide, blunt shield.

The monstrous creature erupted from the void, huge jaws gaping, revealing rows of long black teeth. It missed the wagon by inches, smashing into the shield and exploding to angry tatters of mist.

Eliath pulled with every ounce of his strength, trying to gauge where the next attack might come from.

The far side of the gorge was just ahead!

Eliath stopped short. Something stood at the end of the bridge, blocking the path. A figure covered in black armor, faceplate drawn, stepped forward. In a black-gloved hand, the dark knight held a staff of power. The jewel upon its tip glowed dangerously.

Eliath drew the sword strapped to his back. Ancient Elvin magic coursed up and down its fine edges.

The dark knight raised his staff, sending its foul magic into the mists.

A mistbeast sprang from the gorge, sinking teeth into wood. With a vicious shake of its massive head, it ripped out the rear wheels. The wagon fell backward, crashing to the stone and sliding half over the edge.

Eliath instantly threw the amulet. The glittering shield expanded, wrapping around the wagon.

The startled centaur suddenly felt his neck locked in an iron grip.

Eliath desperately struggled to stand his ground, but the knight was too strong. With a cry, the brave centaur was thrown into the void.

The wagon lurched, teetering perilously on the edge of the bridge.

The knight's armor-clad hand grasped only mist as the wagon tumbled into the gorge.

Blinding light exploded, spreading into a wide circle inside the clouds.

With a last burst, the light vanished, taking the terrified screams with it.

Chapter 1

The mistwolf's howl rang across the bright examination room of the Stonehill Animal Hospital. Dr. Carolyn Fletcher dodged the pup's thrashing tail as she handed the syringe to her thirteen-year-old daughter, Emily. The wolf turned and snarled.

"Watch your manners!" Adriane scolded. The dark-haired girl, Emily's friend, was struggling to hold the squirming pup in place.

Adriane had a special bond with the young mistwolf; she was his pack mate. His name was Dreamer. The mistwolf locked his emerald gaze into Adriane's dark eyes. The image of a long, sharp needle entered Adriane's mind.

"I know, but it's for your own good," Adriane read Dreamer's mind and reassured the mistwolf pup.

"Good boy, you're almost done." Dr. Fletcher ran her hands over his lustrous fur, checking for abrasions or marks.

Dreamer wriggled under the vet's touch, his front paws sliding off the examination table.

"Emily, help Adriane get him on the scale."

Emily deposited the syringe in a disposal bin and put her arms around Dreamer's midsection. "Easy, Dreamer, this won't hurt. I promise." Emily's rainbow healing stone set inside her silver bracelet pulsed soft blue as she sent waves of calm at the growling pup. She and Adriane wrangled him onto the scale.

"Stop being such a big baby," Adriane said gently.

"Big is right," Dr. Fletcher said, adjusting the weights.

"Thirty pounds already?" Emily's hazel eyes widened. "He's only three months old."

"Hand me his chart, Emily," Dr. Fletcher studied the scale.

A small, furry paw pushed the folder toward Carolyn's outstretched hand.

Emily grabbed the chart and glared at the golden brown ferret standing on a stool behind her mother.

"Just being helpful," Ozzie said, smiling. His paw rested proudly on a bright golden stone secured to a leather collar. Though most people believed he was just a remarkable ferret, Ozzie

was actually an elf. He had been sent to Earth disguised in a ferret's body by the Fairimentals, the guardians of his magical home world of Aldenmor. Since receiving the ferret stone from the Fairimentals for his bravery, he'd been using it nonstop to chatter telepathically with his friends who had their own magic jewels.

"With all that special puppy chow *someone's* been ordering via e-mail," Carolyn said, eyeing her daughter. "It's no wonder Dreamer's not full grown by now."

"E-mail orders?" Emily gave Ozzie a glower.

"Er, they had a special on beef bits and liver snaps," Ozzie said.

"Dreamer will need another immunization in six months," Dr. Fletcher told Adriane. "He's perfectly healthy, and a magnificent animal."

Adriane smiled. "Hear that?" she asked, attaching Dreamer's collar, a black leather and turquoise band she had made to match the one around her wrist.

"He's going to be well over 100 pounds," Dr. Fletcher continued, her brow furrowed in concern.

"And he's like nothing I've ever seen before."

Dr. Fletcher was more right than she realized. This was no ordinary wolf. Dreamer was a mistwolf, an animal native to the magical world of Aldenmor. No longer was he the scraggly, scared orphan he had been just a short time ago when Adriane, Emily, and their friend Kara had found him. Under Adriane's care, his jet-black coat gleamed like velvet, rippling over streamlined muscles, built to run. Green eyes that had been dark with fear now shone like twin emerald pools. A snow-white star gleamed on his chest, and each paw was banded in white, as if he ran on clouds.

"Adriane's been working really hard training him," Emily said.

"Even with the best of training, he's a wild animal, and at some point might need to be cared for by specialists, for his own safety as well as yours," her mom advised them.

As if trying to prove her right, Dreamer made a break for it, nails screeching against the metal scale. Adriane grabbed and held him.

"You've both been doing a great job with Ravenswood, but it's my job to monitor the animals for the town council. We still don't know what's become of Stormbringer," Dr. Fletcher said.

Emily caught the quick flare from Adriane's golden wolf stone along with a sharp wince of pain. Stormbringer had been a beautiful silver mistwolf bonded to Adriane. During the battle

14

with the Dark Sorceress, the evil half-animal, half-human magic master, Storm had sacrificed herself to save all of Aldenmor's mistwolves. The pain of losing her former pack mate was still very fresh, and Emily worried constantly that Adriane was keeping too much inside.

"And you!" Dr. Fletcher swung around and grabbed Ozzie, plunking the startled ferret on the scale. "You've gained six whole ounces in less than a month!"

"Hee-hee."

"I'm putting you on a strict diet!"

"*Gah!*" Ozzie exclaimed, and was about to protest when Emily quickly covered his mouth.

"Mom, it's your fault for giving him lasagna." Emily poked Ozzie's round belly.

"*Lasagna! I need that!*" the ferret squealed.

"From now on, it's diet lasagna." Dr. Fletcher smiled, patting the ferret's head. "Who's the best ferret in the world?"

Ozzie pointed to himself, cracking Carolyn up. Emily sighed.

"Oh, and Emily," Carolyn said seriously, "you need to call your dad back and let him know what you've decided about winter break."

"Yeah, I know,' Emily mumbled, her long curly hair falling over downturned eyes. Her dad had asked her to join him and his new wife on a vacation out west. She had tried not to think about it.

"Come on," Adriane said, slipping into her vest. "We have some hungry animals that aren't as lucky as the chubby ferret."

"Hey!" Ozzie said. *"I resemble that remark!"*

      ❧   ❧   ❧

Patches of snow glinted white in the noonday light, making Emily squint as she crunched down the frozen path through Owl Creek Bird Sanctuary, one of her favorite spots on the Ravenswood Preserve. She watched diamond flakes drifting to and fro between thick, towering trunks of maples and oak. Rows of pine, hundreds thick, resplendent in their winter greens, lined the distant ice-crested shores of the Chitakaway River.

The comfort she normally took from this place had little effect today. She was upset with her dad for marrying a woman she didn't even know. But there was more to what she was feeling. Emily and her two friends, Adriane and Kara, were mages, users of magic, but they were young and inexperienced, with profound responsibilities placed upon them. Emily was a healer, Adriane a warrior, and Kara a blazing star.

During their battle against the Dark Sorceress, the mages had released healing magic from Avalon, the hidden home of all magic. They hadn't heard anything from any of their friends on Aldenmor in weeks. The portal in the Ravenswood field had just seemed to vanish, leaving only nagging questions.

What did it really mean to be a mage? How long could they keep the secret? What were they supposed to do now?

"Over here, slowpokes," Adriane called out. She was hoisting a bag from a wooden shed, one of many feed stations set among the trails of the preserve. Already several hawks, peacocks, and white-tailed deer had gathered, waiting for the young caretakers.

Emily marveled at Adriane's strength and courage. A healer could only fix things after they were broken. She wished she could take action, be a warrior like her friend.

"You know, it's seventy degrees in New Mexico today," Ozzie said, snuggled in the deep front pocket of Emily's parka.

"Maybe you'll like her," Adriane said, spreading the feed into several wide troughs.

"I hate her!" Emily blurted before she could think. "They eloped and didn't even invite me to the wedding."

"They probably didn't want to make a big deal about getting married," Adriane guessed.

"I already have a mom!" Emily swallowed, suppressing the hot ache in her throat. "I don't need some *stepmom* telling me what to do."

Before Adriane could answer, Dreamer sent a mental image of forest underbrush and a pair of big ears.

Adriane frowned at the interruption. "You're a mistwolf, not a dog. You can talk if you want to tell me something."

"Rabbit!" Dreamer said impatiently.

"This is an animal preserve. You can't eat rabbits!" Her dark eyes flashed with exasperation.

"Just have a little patience with him," Emily said soothingly, instantly forgetting her own problems.

"I've tried! Your mom is right, Dreamer's just getting wilder all the time. Storm never acted like this."

Emily's heart ached for her friend. Adriane's bond with Stormbringer had been deeper than they could have ever imagined. That was the way with magical animals. Once bonded, it was a true friendship meant to last a lifetime.

In response to his pack mate's distress, Dreamer leaped onto the path, scattering the animals with a loud growl.

"Dreamer, no!" Adriane shouted. "They're not hurting me."

Emily tried to calm the frightened animals as Adriane settled Dreamer down.

The mistwolf sat and projected an image of the needle, as if its medicine could help Adriane.

"It's not the same thing," the dark-haired girl tried to explain as she knelt to stroke the wolf. "Sometimes you just hurt inside."

Dreamer gave her face a lick.

She smiled. "Thank you, yes, that's better." Adriane rose and faced Emily. "Sometimes I wish I could be a healer mage like you."

Emily took Adriane's hands in hers. Blue light from the rainbow jewel mixed with sparks of golden fire from Adriane's wolf stone, reinforcing the bond between healer and warrior.

"Hoooo!"

A white owl barreled from the sky right toward Emily's head. The red-haired girl instantly stretched her arm out—and the bird made a perfect landing, wings shimming with gold, turquoise, and lavender.

"What is it, Ariel?" Emily asked.

"Come quickly," the owl said. *"Blazing star out of control."*

"I left her in the library," Ozzie said. "How much damage could she possibly do?"

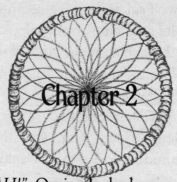

Chapter 2

"*GAH!*" Ozzie ducked as a flying book smacked into the library wall. The Ravenswood Library was a whirlwind of motion as dozens of books careened in all directions at once. Adriane and Emily swung the door fully open, knocking the ferret onto another diving leather-bound tome. Ozzie was whisked high into the air.

Dreamer dashed inside and chomped a low-flying journal. Shaking it furiously, shredded pages fluttered around him like snow.

"Dreamer, no!" Adriane ran inside, dodging a large bookend shaped like a dragon. She raised her arm, instantly releasing a wave of gold from her jewel. She spun the light into a broad shield to protect herself and Emily from the myriad of flying objects.

Under a wide table, a large gold leopard-spotted cat, Lyra, huddled next to a pegasus called Balzathar. The cat had unfurled magical golden wings to cover Ronif and Rasha, two ducklike quiffles.

"Mage gone wild," Balthazar warned, swatting a book away with his tail.

"Thank goodness we're rescued," Ronif said, popping out from under Lyra's shimmering wing. His mate quickly caught the quiffle as he was lifted in the air by the magical forces.

"Kara?" Emily shouted, shielding her face as a screaming ferret whooshed by.

"Up here!" a voice called out.

Hunkered under Adriane's golden shield, Emily made her way past the huge mobile hanging from the domed ceiling. Suns, moons, and planets swung in concentric circles.

The spacious library occupied several top floors of Ravenswood Manor and was lined with racks of shelves to store the wealth of books. High atop the tallest bookshelf sat a blond-haired girl with a crystalline jewel sparking erratically from her necklace.

"How did you get up there?" Emily asked.

Kara pointed. The tall, rolling ladder was making its way around the far side of the library, barreling straight for the mages.

Adriane whipped the shield into a rope, ensnaring the ladder and pulling it to a stop next to Kara.

"Thanks, Indy." Kara daintily climbed down,

holding the book she had retrieved, oblivious to the chaos.

"Kara!"

"Yes?" She looked up, blinking her light blue eyes.

Adriane and Emily each extended an arm, indicating the magical mess.

"Oh, that." Kara closed her eyes and held up her unicorn jewel. The flying objects suddenly crashed to the floor in crumpled heaps. Dreamer yelped and dove under the table, scattering the other animals like bowling pins. Ozzie's book skidded atop the table, sending the ferret flying into a furry heap on the couch.

"Fascinating." Kara Davies's blue eyes sparkled happily as she read from the book. "Did you know that amulets and talismans date back to cavemen?"

"A monkey couldn't have made a bigger mess," Adriane said angrily.

Kara rolled her eyes.

"I could use a protection amulet," Lyra complained, green eyes glinting as she stretched her lithe body.

Kara stuck her tongue out turning it green for a split second. She had absorbed her new shapeshifting abilities from one of the Dark Sorceress's minions, a skultum, after defeating the fairy creature in a battle of wits.

"We're supposed to practice together," Adriane warned. "You know what happens when you use magic, everything goes crazy!"

"Oh, this is nothing. I'll fix it in a jiffy," Kara said, raising her sparkling jewel.

"No!" Everyone in the room yelled at once.

"Whatever." Kara slumped in a chair and read from her book.

"Kara, you know you have to be careful with your jewel," Emily lectured. "We have no idea what it's capable of."

"How am I supposed to find out if I don't use it?" Kara pouted.

"It's obviously very powerful, so we should all be together when you do—just in case, okay?" Emily reminded her.

"Okay, okay."

Ozzie scampered to a leather chair and used his jewel to open a secret sliding bookcase. Hidden behind was the Ravenswood computer. The computer stored all sorts of magical information and allowed the mages access to their website. Ozzie immediately began pounding away at the keys, sorting the latest e-mails for the girls to answer later.

"So what's with the long faces?" Kara asked, peering over the top of her book.

"Emily has to decide if she's going to New Mexico," Adriane answered.

"You can't avoid meeting her forever, you know," Kara said to Emily. "She'll think you don't care."

"She obviously doesn't care what I think," Emily shot back. "I'm not dropping everything and going all the way cross-country just to meet her."

"Isn't your dad going, too?" Kara asked, eyes twinkling.

"Funny!" Emily scoffed. Then she added, "Yeah, I really want to see him."

"So, there you go."

"It's not that easy."

"Yes, it is. Three simple words: Get over it." Kara rolled her ice-blue eyes.

"That is *so* not helpful, Miss Overachiever," Adriane said.

Kara extended her fingers into claws and morphed her face into a horrid image of a wizened banshee.

"Keep it up, princess," Adriane laughed. "Maybe your face will freeze like that."

Kara's eyes widened, and she quickly morphed back, checking her face in the wall mirror to make sure.

"Here it is, Emily," Ozzie called out. "The Four Winds Resort, located in sunny Carlsbad, New Mexico."

Emily and Adriane walked to the computer and glanced over the ferret's head.

"Wow, check out these desert pics!" Adriane exclaimed, hitting some of the links. "And right next door is the Happy Trails Horse Ranch. It would be so awesome to ride horses for a whole week!"

"If you think it sounds so great, you go," Emily muttered. She stopped short, her own words giving her an idea. "Hey, you *should* come with me."

"I dunno," Adriane responded. "How would I afford it?"

"I'll ask my dad," Emily said excitedly. "I'm sure he'll cover it."

"What about our chores here?"

"Balthazar, Ronif, and I can handle that," Rasha quickly put in.

"Well, what about Dreamer?"

"He's still small enough for a transport cage. Pleeeeeeze, Adriane!!! You've got to go. I'm not going unless you do," Emily insisted.

Adriane thought for a minute, then turned to Kara. "What about you, Goldilocks?"

"Send me a postcard. As of today, there're only two weeks left before the Valentine's Day dance!"

Kara began counting off on her pink-polished fingers. "I have to get the band, arrange for the decorations, find the perfect dress, get my hair done, a manicure, a pedicure, a—"

"Fine," Emily said, hitting a link on the screen. "We'll check out the spa without you."

Kara's blue eyes opened wide. "What spa?" Dropping her book, she leaped to her feet and crammed between Adriane and Emily, reading the computer screen.

"The Fours Winds is home to the world-famous health and beauty spa . . . ," Kara read, suddenly radiating with enthusiasm. "Honey-infused facemasks, exotic kelp wraps, mud baths, complexion massages! I'm in."

"What about your ball, Sleeping Beauty?" Adriane asked.

"After a week at the Four Winds, I'll totally be the belle of the ball!"

"Nature hikes, desert tours, horseback riding—they have it all!" Adriane added.

"Girl, we are going to have so much fun!" Kara squealed.

"I'm shocked," Adriane suddenly stated.

"Why?" Kara asked, checking her sweater for stains.

"This might be the first time we've agreed on

anything," Adriane laughed, and gave Kara a high five.

Looking at her friends' eager faces, doubt gnawed at Emily. "Guys, what about the . . . you know." She held up her wrist, the rainbow jewel catching glints of light. "What if we're needed on Aldenmor?"

"We don't know what's happening on Aldenmor!" Kara jumped away from the computer. "We did our job, so let the Fairimentals do theirs. It's time for us to get back to our normal lives." She wagged a long purple finger.

"Normal, huh?" Adriane arched an eyebrow.

"Oops." Kara quickly changed her digit back. "Besides, the Fairimentals have a knack for finding us if there's an emergency."

Emily realized her friends were right. With the Ravenswood portal closed, there was nothing they could do for the Fairimentals for the time being.

She'd have to meet her dad's new wife sometime, and she'd rather have her friends by her side when it happened.

"All right," the red-haired girl said. "I'll let my dad know."

"Wait a minute!" Ozzie shouted, nose plastered against the monitor. "New Mexico is 'the Land of Enchantment.' Are there wizards there?"

"That's just the state motto, silly," Emily laughed.

"Yeah, the only thing you have to worry about are aliens," Adriane said, pointing to the Roswell link.

"Aliens?" the ferret gulped.

"Those are just stories, Ozzie," Kara said, "like dragons and trolls and, uh, okay, so we've actually *seen* all of those."

Ozzie narrowed his eyes and looked at each of the girls in turn. "Somehow I get the feeling this is going to be quite an adventure."

Chapter 3

*H*elp! TooPH! It's dark in here—CroooOP—You
stepped on my tail! Where are we?—EEEooo-
eeoop—that smells!

A jumble of sounds and voices echoed in
Emily's mind. She shut her eyes, blocking out the
mental barrage. She seemed to be picking up a
magical transmission. But what could be calling to
her in New Mexico?

She paced outside a big red barn as crowds of
happy tourists gathered inside. The Happy Trails
Horse Ranch was a series of stables, corrals, picnic
grounds, and low-rise buildings sprawled across
several acres of desert. Emily shaded her eyes as
she scanned the Four Winds Resort about three
hundred yards up a dirt road. The complex glis-
tened like a glass-and-chrome oasis complete with
landscaped gardens and fountains.

She watched Dreamer and Adriane running
along the dusty road leading from the resort to the

ranch. The wolf, ecstatic finally to be outside, was sniffing and exploring everything in sight.

"I still don't hear anything," Ozzie said, his eyes squeezed shut as he gripped his jewel. He was sitting in Emily's backpack. "What's it sound like?"

"It's weird, like a jumbled radio," she admitted. As soon as they'd landed, she'd heard it: tingling snippets of sounds rippling through her mind.

Her senses always increased exponentially by the magic of her healing stone. Like her past experiences, these feelings were unfocused, like a half-remembered melody echoing across the desert. At least she didn't get sick anymore.

"I can't get Dreamer to calm down. Can you help?" Adriane called, approaching as Dreamer pulled and chewed on the leash.

Emily kneeled to rub Dreamer's head. At her touch, he instantly calmed, looking deep into the healer's eyes. Waves of sparkling colors floated across Emily's mind. "You feel it too, don't you?" she asked the mistwolf.

A low growl slipped between Dreamer's teeth. *"Magic."*

"Magic? Out here?" Adriane asked, startled. "You sure?"

Dreamer nodded. He was a natural magic

tracker, and Adriane had worked especially hard honing the mistwolf's skills.

"I think an animal is in trouble," Emily explained.

Adriane examined her amber wolf stone. "I don't sense any danger."

"Gather round, cowpokes!" boomed a deep voice from inside the barn.

"Any sign of your dad yet?" Adriane asked.

"No." Emily was almost glad her dad was late. She needed time to pull herself together before dealing with her new stepmom.

"Come on, we're going to miss the welcome speech," Adriane said, hitting the retractable leash, pulling Dreamer close.

The three walked into the cool shade of the large barn. Inside, guests gathered in the wide center, about twenty-five kids, teens, and adults. On the far side, Kara stood chatting away with a dark-haired woman, well dressed in an expensive Western skirt, silk shirt, and jacket.

Kara laughed and chatted with the woman as if they were old friends.

Leave it to Kara, Emily thought. Making friends already with a mannequin from some well-dressed Western fashion catalog.

"Whoo-hoo!" A tall, burly man stood in the

center of the barn, whooping. He was dressed in full cowboy gear, from his hat, boots, and bolo tie down to a big brass belt buckle with a bucking bronco. "Lemme hear you, now! Come on, let's do some whoopin'!"

The group gave a cursory whoop.

"Naw, that's a city slicker whoop. We need a real Texas whoop!" He smiled.

The group whooped louder. Dreamer threw his head back and howled, startling everyone.

"Dreamer!" Adriane hissed, struggling to untangle the wolf from his leash.

"That's the ticket. Name's Texas Slim. And I welcome ya'll to the Happy Trails Horse Ranch. For the next five days you're gonna be livin' the life of cowboys and cowgirls. Ridin' horses, explorin' the desert, cookouts . . ."

PhoooBB! Move over! Faaahtooot!

Emily looked sharply around her. "Ozzie, did you hear that?"

"No, I can't get my stupid stone to do anything," Ozzie whispered, shaking his ferret stone.

Emily moved away from the crowd to try to get a sharper impression from the strange sounds. Shining saddles sat on stands, and bridles hung from wall hooks as she walked past a row of stalls. An image of carrots suddenly popped into her mind. Where did that come from? She looked at the nearest stall. A black-and-white-splotched pony stared at her with beautiful liquid eyes.

Emily petted its velveteen muzzle, half listening to Texas Slim's speech.

"Some of y'all might be in the Southwest for the first time. It's prettier than a painted peach, but there's an old sayin' 'bout these parts: Everythin' in the desert is gonna try to bite, sting, or scratch you, and sometimes all at once . . ."

Emily scratched the pony's soft ear. "I'm sorry, I don't have any carrots for you."

"How'd you know carrots are Domino's favorite?"

A pretty teenage girl with short, dark brown hair and dark eyes slipped out of the neighboring stall. She quickly latched the wooden door before a white-and-reddish-brown-spotted pony could follow her out.

"I'm Sierra Sanchez." The girl took a carrot from the pocket of her brown suede vest and handed it to Emily.

"Hi, I'm Emily Fletcher." The healer took the carrot and smiled.

"You're from the Ravenswood Preserve," Sierra said as Domino eagerly devoured the carrot from Emily's palm.

"Yes, how did you know?" Emily was startled.

"Ravenswood is *so* cool. I've been to your website," Sierra said excitedly. "When I saw your name on the guest list, I practically freaked. We have a lot in common. I'm a guide here."

"My friends Adriane and Kara are here, too," Emily said. "And Ozzie."

The ferret leaned toward Sierra and pointed to his mouth.

"He's adorable!"

"And hungry."

"She's a beautiful paint pony," Emily quickly said, stroking Domino's head as she gave Ozzie a stern look.

"You know your horses," Sierra said approvingly, feeding another carrot chunk to the pony in the stall next to Domino. "I've ridden paints my whole life, mostly this gelding here. His name's Apache . . ."

Sierra's words faded. Loneliness, fear, and confusion filled Emily's senses.

Something felt so familiar—

". . . beautiful bracelet. Are you all right?" Sierra asked, glancing at Emily's wrist.

"Just a little jet lag," Emily smiled weakly, covering her glittering jewel with her shirtsleeve.

"Emily, twelve o' clock," Adriane's voice popped in her head.

At the barn doors, a man stood waving.

"Excuse me, Sierra, I see my dad," Emily said.

Forgetting about everything, she began running—and stopped short. His wave had not been for her.

Oh no! The woman talking to Kara was waving back to her dad.

Emily watched in horror as he walked to the woman and gave her a kiss. She stood frozen as she watched Kara point right toward her.

David Fletcher's hazel eyes, the exact color of Emily's, widened as he caught sight of his daughter. "Em!"

He ran over and caught her in a big bear hug, just like he used to do.

"Daddy!" Emily hugged him back, tears leaking from her eyes.

"Emily, sweetheart, look how you've grown." He held her at arm's length, eyes also damp. "You're so beautiful!"

Emily smiled self-consciously, trying to tame her long red curls. She and her dad hugged again. She felt the familiar comfort from his presence, and her heart soared.

"You look good, too, Dad," Emily said truthfully. He *did* look good. He had thinned down, and his warm, friendly eyes and strong brow were framed by neatly trimmed curly hair.

"*Gah!*" Ozzie had wedged himself firmly between Emily and her dad.

"Oh, sorry, little guy!" David let Emily go and patted the ferret. "This must be Ozzie! A little chubbier than I thought."

The ferret covered his stomach with his paws and scowled.

"You missed the orientation," Emily told him.

"Sorry, Em. I had to register and get the bags to the rooms," he explained, smiling at the dark-haired girl who had joined them. "You must be Adriane. I've heard so much about you, I feel you're a real part of the family."

"Thank you," Adriane said, beaming. "This is Dreamer."

"Hey Boy." David leaned to ruffle the pup's scruff.

Emily saw the dark-haired woman straighten her suede jacket and step forward. Edging past Dreamer, she pushed her flowing hair into place with perfectly manicured nails.

"Emily, this is Veronica," David began.

"Emily, darling!" Veronica grabbed Emily in a hug, then looked her over as if appraising a piece of furniture. Her smile revealed faultlessly white teeth framed by glossy red lips. "Your dad has told me so much about you."

"Hi," Emily muttered. She felt Veronica's eyes

canvassing every part of her, from her wild curly hair to her denim shirt and jeans.

Emily felt woozy.

"Em, are you okay?" her dad asked.

Focusing on the dark auburn of his hair, she nodded. "Just a little tired from the trip."

"I've had the most precious time with your friend Kara. She is just the best!" Veronica's pale skin seemed too white.

Emily nodded mutely, watching Kara's beaming smile.

"I just *love* those boots, Veronica!" the blazing star said, admiring the woman's stylish beige suede boots. "Where did you ever find those?"

"Paris, hon." Veronica winked. "Perks of being a curator. The galleries I represent send me to Europe a few times a year."

"That is *so* cool!" Kara gushed. "Isn't it, Em?"

Emily managed a faint smile thinking: Someone get me out of this nightmare.

Dreamer sniffed Veronica curiously. She frowned, brushing mistwolf slobber off her purse.

"Hey!" David said excitedly. "Guess what, girls? I managed to reserve a cabin just for the three of you."

"A cabin!" Adriane beamed.

"A *cabin*?" Kara wailed. "We're not staying at the resort?"

"Veronica and I are. We figured you girls would have more fun at the horse ranch. Isn't that great?"

"Cool! Thanks, Mr. Fletcher," Adriane said.

"Yippee-kay-yae," Kara said sarcastically.

Veronica pulled a slip of paper from her purse and smiled. "I have a pass to the spa for you, Emily. I thought we could spend some quality bonding time in the mud bath."

Mud bath! I'm not a flobbin! Emily thought, aghast.

"I'm not big on spas," she managed, clenching her teeth. "Kara might like it, though."

Kara was practically salivating.

"Well, if Emily doesn't feel like using it, you can certainly join me instead, Kara."

"Giddyyup!" the blonde whooped.

"So how you fine folks doing?" Texas Slim asked as he approached, grinning broadly. Sierra was at his side.

"*Ooof!*" Veronica stumbled as Dreamer side-swiped her.

"That's some hound dog you got there."

"He's a dingo," Kara said quickly, earning a sharp look from Adriane.

"Your daughter's already met my niece Sierra," Texas said to David and his new wife. "Best darn horse wrangler in four states."

Sierra's eyebrows rose at the sight of the huge "dingo."

"I'm Kara and I love your pendant," the blond girl said, stepping forward and smiling. "Turquoise is always *so* in."

"Perfect accessory for any outfit," Veronica added, smiling at Kara.

Emily looked at the beautiful gemstone that hung from Sierra's neck. Why hadn't she noticed that before?

"Thanks. It's been in my family for generations." Sierra touched the bright turquoise oval suspended by a thick silver chain. "Your gems are really cool, too."

Kara proudly held out her sparkling unicorn jewel. "I found mine in a little place over the rainbow—"

The unicorn jewel suddenly popped with diamond light. Startled, Kara jumped back.

"Kara, where did you get such an outrageous fashion statement?" Veronica giggled in delight. "I love it!"

Emily looked at Kara's jeans. The blazing star's belt had turned into a pink feather boa.

"Never did understand fashion." Texas Slim shook his head.

"Um, it's the latest thing," Kara explained quickly. "Belts that change from casual to casual-er. They're still working out the bugs—"

Sierra's brow furrowed suspiciously.

"Listen up, everyone!" Texas Slim waved his hat in the air. "I'm gonna be leadin' a hike to the Arrow Rocks drawings just a yodel south of the resort, and Sierra's leadin' a trail ride to Echo Ridge, a holler or so up north. That's a lot of beautiful country to see. So let's get crackin'."

"Emily, come on my trail ride," Sierra pleaded. "Domino would love it."

"Okay, I guess."

"Great, see you guys later," Sierra said, heading back to the stalls.

"We're going to check out the hotel. Dinner's at six," David said, giving Emily a hug. "It was great to finally meet everyone. Have fun!"

Veronica's hand slipped into David's arm, pulling him away.

"Your stepmom is so awesome!" Kara raved. "What?"

Adriane glared at Kara. "What are you doing?!"

Kara squeezed her eyes shut and changed her belt back into brown Gucci leather. "I didn't do anything!"

40

"Keep your magic in check," Adriane warned the blond girl sternly. "We've got a situation."

"I'll say. I'm not sleeping in a log cabin."

"You can sleep in a tree if you want, but I was referring to Emily."

Kara noticed the tight lines of distress on her friend's face. "Emily, what's wrong?"

Taking a deep breath, Emily told the blazing star, "I think there's a magical animal in trouble."

Kara looked around. She'd been through enough with the mages to trust Emily's intuition about animals and magic. "Here?"

Dreamer barked in agreement, sending an image of the desert.

"Somewhere out there," Emily said.

"What do we do?" Kara asked.

"Okay, huddle up," Adriane ordered. The three mages leaned forward, heads touching. Ozzie scrunched in between with Dreamer in the center.

"Here's the play," Adriane said. "I'll go on Texas Slim's hike and let Dreamer do some scouting. You ready for that?"

Dreamer nodded affirmatively.

"Good boy. Emily, you go on Sierra's trail ride and canvas the area. You find anything, you let us know right away."

Kara clutched the free pass in her hand like it was a magic gem. "And I will check out the spa!"

"Fine. But no one goes near anything unusual without the others. Okay?"

"Hike!" Kara exclaimed as the three mages clasped hands, fuzzy ferret paw on top, wet wolf nose underneath.

"And no more magic, Dorothy!" Adriane said to Kara.

"Okay, okay," Kara bit her lip and fingering her stone nervously.

"Don't you worry, Emily," Ozzie said. "We'll find whoever it is."

"I know we will, Ozzie," Emily whispered, her senses reeling. That was just what she was afraid of.

Chapter 4

The group of eight riders marveled at the sun-bleached desert stretching to the horizon. Contrasting starkly with the panorama of muted yellows, browns, greens, and silvers, the brilliant azure sky soared overhead.

The riders had stopped at Echo Ridge lookout to view the perfect picture postcard vista.

"We're in the Guadalupe Mountain Range," Sierra said, pointing to the bronze mountains rising like majestic towers. "In the middle of the Chihuahuan Desert. Although it looks dry and parched, it's teeming with life if you know where to look."

As if in response to Sierra's words, a gaggle of twittering quails skittered between nearby cacti.

"Easy, girl," Emily said, patting Domino's neck.

The mare shifted anxiously, sensing Emily's concern. Something was definitely reaching out to her, drifting across the wide-open space like tumbleweed. Even Ozzie's ferret stone was reacting, flashing erratically with golden light. The ferret sat in front of Emily, braced against the saddlehorn. With one paw to his brow, he surveyed the land while holding his stone out in the other paw like a homing beacon.

Sierra moved among the group, offering advice to the novice riders, tightening stirrups and bridles.

Although Emily hadn't ridden in years, Domino seemed to make it so easy for her. She closed her eyes and took a deep breath. Her senses filled with sweet, dry, desert air, the smell of leather, and the heft of Domino's strong smooth muscles beneath her.

I'm hungry! FooB! I'm scared. I'm itchy. I'm more itchy!

Who said that?

Startled, Emily turned to a canyon running about a mile east of the lookout. The reds, beiges, browns, and purples of the ridgeline swept into the enclosed space.

"Ozzie?" She nodded her head toward the voices.

He swung his ferret stone toward the canyon walls, and it glowed deep gold. "Yes, definitely over there."

"I'm going to try to contact whoever it is."

"Right!" Ozzie held his ferret stone close to the healing stone upon Emily's wrist.

She closed her eyes and reached with her mind. *"Hello. Can you hear me?"*

PooT?

"My name is Emily. I'm a healer mage."

PHHOOOOLLL! BoooF-FrOOOth! PaWOooO!

Emily's mind was bombarded with overwhelming noise. She gasped, covering her ears.

"Are you all right, Emily?"

Emily opened her eyes to see Sierra swinging Apache around beside her.

"Er, yes, I'm okay," she answered. "What's that canyon over there?" Emily pointed east.

"That's Pecos Canyon. It's part of Carlsbad Caverns which run throughout these mountains. They're world famous for deep caves. Just don't ever go inside without an experienced spelunker."

"A what?"

"A cave explorer," Sierra explained. "You could wander about for days and never find a way out."

Emily eyed the canyon worriedly. "You'll probably think I'm crazy, but I think there's an animal in trouble there."

Sierra's eyes widened. "How do you know that?"

Emily frowned, not wanting to say too much. "Something doesn't feel right to me."

Instead of questioning Emily further, Sierra called to the others, "Everyone stay here. Emily and I are going to check something out."

The group, grateful for the chance to ease their sore behinds, cheered.

Apache snorted and took off at a gallop.

Domino followed, allowing Emily to adjust to a canter before breaking into full gallop. The paint moved in perfect harmony with her rider.

The two horses sliced a wake of dust as they made their way down the sloping trail. They soon found the entrance to the canyon.

"Hold up," Sierra called, slowing Apache to a walk.

Brown and red desert sands of the canyon floor stretched before them, surrounded by high-striated walls. They reminded Emily of sand sculptures she had seen, layered with pastel colors.

"We'll do a quick pass through and head back," Sierra said.

"Thank you," Emily said gratefully, letting Domino lead the way.

"You've always had a way with animals?" Sierra wondered.

"I grew up around them. My mom's a vet."

"Ah, that explains it." She nodded toward Domino. "I've never seen Domino so taken with a rider before."

"She's the best, Sierra. I just love her," Emily said, patting the horse's neck.

Domino nickered, radiating waves of pleasure.

"What about you, Sierra? I mean, you seem so in touch with the land."

"Before I left Mexico to live with Uncle Tex, my grandpa gave me this jewel." Sierra fingered her turquoise pendant. "He said it had special powers that only I could use."

Emily could have sworn the turquoise jewel pulsed just then. It must have caught a reflection of sunlight.

"Emily, I wanted to ask about your jewels."

The healer stiffened.

"Each of your friends has one. Even Ozzie. I read on your site that sometimes jewels have . . . properties."

"Yes, that's true. They focus different types of energy."

"Sometimes mine helps me see things, feel things . . . differently. I can sense things about the desert," Sierra said as her attention was drawn to a solitary dune rising from the center of the canyon floor.

"What is it, Sierra?" Emily asked, eyeing the strange mound.

"I don't know. But it wasn't here last week."

"Emily, look," Ozzie said, pointing to the ground.

Splintered wooden planks littered the sand as they approached the mysterious mound.

They were practically on top of it before they realized what they were looking at—the wreckage of a fancy carriage. The size of a bus, it was face-down, half buried in the sand. The rear axle was broken, one back wheel ripped to pieces. Broken wood surrounded a gnarly hole in its side where a large chunk of the wagon was missing.

Sierra pulled back on Apache's reins and slid effortlessly to the ground. Emily dismounted, set Ozzie on the sand, and joined Sierra by the wreckage.

A burst of wind made the single whole wheel creak in a slow circle.

"There's nothing inside," Emily said peering into the open hole.

She looked closer. Deep rents scarred the richly grained wood—teeth marks. Running her fingers over the serrated slashes, Emily shivered, suddenly feeling cold in the bright afternoon sun. Whatever had made those marks was big.

"And there are no tracks." Sierra swept her arm over the surrounding area. "It's as if the thing just fell from the sky."

"Emily, look at this!" Ozzie was digging into the dirt where the front of the wagon lay submerged.

It was a section of polished wood. Ornate symbols were carved in a brass plate.

"It's some kind of academy crest," he explained.

"You mean this is like a school bus?" Emily asked.

"Yes, I think so."

"Then what kind of students was it carrying?"

Mage? Are you there? Shhh, quiet! How do we know it's a mage and not a werebeast? Oooot, you're right—gimme that—No, that's my last sunbeam cracker!

The magic hit Emily like a fist. She gasped, eyes drawn to the sheer canyon face in front of them. Several cave openings riddled the base. It was coming from inside one of them. And now she had no doubt.

"Ozzie, it feels like unicorn magic," Emily told the ferret.

"Unicorns? You sure?"

"Yes. I think there are unicorns here—and I think they are in trouble."

Ozzie knew as well as the mages that unicorns were the most powerful of all magical creatures—and the most coveted by those who desired magic. The mages had fought for them before, rescuing a unicorn named Lorelei from the Dark Sorceress and saving the unicorn jewel that had eventually become Kara's.

"We have to get the others and head back," Sierra said, scanning the desert skies. "There's a sandstorm coming, a bad one. If you've sensed an animal here, it's probably a lost bobcat or cougar. They make quite a racket."

The horses pranced nervously as they, too, sensed approaching danger.

"Let's go, Emily," Sierra called as she mounted Apache.

"You start back with Sierra," Ozzie said. *"I'll look in the nearest cave, see if I can confirm a sighting."*

Emily bit her lip. She couldn't risk saying anything else to Sierra. *"Okay. Five minutes, and be careful!"*

The ferret scrambled away and disappeared into the desert.

❧   ❧   ❧

Ozzie crept against the rocky wall near the entrance to a large cave. The ferret kept an eye on his surroundings to make sure nothing was following him. The high sandstone was ribboned with rich earthy shades from pale peach to bright rusty red. Scraggly prickly pear cacti sprouted in clumps, with spiny, paddle-shaped leaves.

"Ahh!" Something bit him! Ozzie leaped and spun around, putting his paws on his ferret stone. Grimacing, he carefully extracted a cactus needle from his fuzzy bottom.

A strong breeze blew through the canyon, sending small pebbles and bits of sandy dirt flying in the air.

"Pa-tooeey!" Ozzie shielded his eyes as the wind grew stronger.

At the far end of the canyon, a whirlwind shimmered into existence and began to take shape. Ozzie blinked—was he really seeing that? Or was it a mirage? But it was no trick of the desert.

The spiral grew larger, pulsing with brilliant colors like a rainbow twisted around itself. The twister touched down on the desert floor, twirling forward like a tornado. Ozzie watched in amazement. Wherever the whirlwind touched, the ground buckled and warped like soft clay.

The dazzling tornado danced over the half-buried wagon. The effect was amazing—brilliant lights shimmered, morphing the wagon into *glistening blue-white ice!*

The whirlwind then wobbled—and headed right for the startled ferret.

"Gah!" Ozzie dove for cover behind a rock outcropping.

The twister coiled overhead in a flurry of color. Inches from his head, the rock morphed into a strange, marshmallowy mass.

An instant later, the whirlwind disappeared, specks of colored magic dissipating like mist.

Ozzie's paws flew to his golden ferret stone. *"Emily! Come in, Emily!"*

"I'm here, Ozzie," the mage answered. *"Did you find something?"*

"Did I?!? You're lucky I'm still a ferret! A weird magic whirlwind just changed a cactus and a rock and the wagon. It nearly got yours truly in the process!"

"Slow down, what are you talking about? A wind?"

"Actually, it was an elemental shift in paramagical forces, to be precise," a new voice broke in.

"GAAAHH! Aliens!!" Ozzie screamed. *"Emily, warn the others, I'l—"*

❧   ❧   ❧

Emily was almost at the sloping trail that led up to Echo Ridge when Ozzie's frazzled voice vanished.

"Ozzie? Ozzie?" Emily called frantically.

There was no answer. Heart thudding, she looked toward the canyon. "Sierra, Ozzie's gotten loose. I need to go look for him."

The brown-haired girl brought Apache up sharp. "Okay, but hurry. I'll round up the others and meet you back here on the trail, but whatever you do, don't go into the caves."

"Okay, I'll be careful," Emily promised.

Domino sensed the mage's urgency and broke

into a gallop, racing back into the canyon. Fear pulsed through Emily's veins. If anything happened to Ozzie, she didn't know what she'd do.

She was halfway across the canyon floor when she realized the wagon was gone. In its place was a large pond of water. Leading Domino to the canyon wall, she searched for Ozzie.

"Give me back my stone or you'll never see your spaceship again!"

Emily turned toward the sound of the ferret's voice. She saw Ozzie hopping up and down on what looked like a pile of twigs.

"Ozzie," Emily said, sliding off Domino and running to her friend, "what are you doing?"

"Interrogating him." Ozzie waved a paw at the twigs. "This alien attacked me!"

Emily looked closer at the mass of twigs, desert grass, and shrubbery. "Ozzie, wait a minute."

The pile suddenly spun and formed into a little wobbly whirlwind.

Crackling and rustling, the tiny whirlwind took another shape before it came to a halt. Slightly shorter than Ozzie, it looked like a little stick figure, made of twigs, dirt, and bushes magically held together. A gray-green clump of sagebrush served as its torso and another as its head. Sparkling eyes of quartz looked at her curiously. Hanging around its neck was a small silver-and-blue gemstone on a chain woven of desert weeds.

"You're a Fairimental!" Emily gasped.

"This thief took my jewel!" Ozzie yelled. "Huh? What the—"

Fairimentals were very powerful and mysterious magical creatures who protected the magic of Aldenmor. Made entirely of elemental magic, they took their physical forms from water, fire, earth, and wind. This one was an earth Fairimental.

The little twig figure stared at Emily's rainbow gem. "You are the Healer?"

Emily nodded. "Yes."

"Oh, thank goodness. I found this mookrat impersonating a mage—does this belong to you?" A spindly branch held out a golden stone.

"That's Ozzie's ferret stone," Emily said.

"Gimme that!" The ferret grabbed his stone and attached it back onto the setting on his collar. "I've met Fairimentals and *they* never robbed me. How do we know you're one?"

"I'm an E.F., and my name is Tweek," the creature said.

"What's an E.F?" Emily asked.

"Experimental Fairimental. I'm the first ever of my kind. The Fairimentals made me at their lab."

"The what from the where?" Ozzie demanded.

"It used to be a place called the Shadowlands,

but now it's a magic preserve and research facility called The Garden. I'm designed to stay on Earth for long periods of time." Fairimentals had visited Emily, Adriane, and Kara on Earth in the past, but their particular magic could only be sustained in this world for minutes, sometimes seconds, before falling apart.

"What are you doing here?" Emily asked.

"I was sent here to find the three mages." Tweek's quartz eyes eyed Ozzie. "*You're* not one, are you?"

"Maybe I am." Ozzie crossed his arms angrily.

"I have a very important message!" Tweek cried, waving his arms so dramatically that a few twigs flew off.

"What is it?" Emily asked worriedly.

Tweek's twiggy features settled into serious lines. "Something terrible has happened. Avalon has lost its magic."

Ozzie pressed his paws to his head. "What!?"

"Can you tell us anything else, Tweek?" Emily asked.

Twigs and branches fell to the ground as the E.F. shuddered. "This is my first assignment," he said, picking up pieces of himself. "Maybe I didn't get everything just right, but I know I have to find the missing magic—AHHHHH!"

Mage and ferret stared at the E.F.

"Look out behind you, it's a—"

BANG! Tweek exploded into a cloud of twigs and brush .

Emily whirled around, her rainbow gem pulsing a deep green warning light.

Four sparkling tornadoes were touching down on the far side of the canyon.

The desert floor bulged and undulated as if it had suddenly turned liquid.

Domino neighed, stomping her hooves, ready to run.

"Let's get out of here!" Ozzie cried.

Grabbing Ozzie, Emily sprang into the saddle as the pony bolted. She had to warn Adriane and Kara. This was no ordinary sandstorm.

"Go, Domino!"

The horse ran at breakneck speed, slaloming around the first whirlwind. The tornado spun like a giant colored top, roaring over rocks and melting them to vile black sludge. Another wind engulfed several cacti, twisting them into horrible thorned monstrosities. Emily leaned left as Domino raced between a pair of oncoming tornadoes, missing them only by a few feet. Stinging edges of dark magic whirled past Emily as her jewel blazed upon her wrist. She stifled a scream. Nature itself was being twisted and bent into unnatural forms. She leaned forward, urging Domino to outrun the fourth wind, leaving the twisters spinning against the canyon walls like pinballs.

Within seconds they were safe, out of the canyon.

Emily looked over her shoulder. Behind them a huge jagged fin rose up and then disappeared beneath the sands.

Chapter 5

Emily walked into her living room. Ghostly beams of light played over what used to be couches and chairs, now twisted into bizarre shapes.

"Emily," Carolyn said, standing in the hallway watching her daughter. "Your new mother is here to see you."

Facing the hearth stood a tall woman, long dark hair falling down her back. The woman turned, and Emily's voice locked in a silent scream.

The woman's porcelain white skin matched the streak of white lightning in her jet-black hair. And her eyes, the vertical slits of an animal, pulsed with a feral glow.

"We're family now, dear," the Dark Sorceress said, beckoning Emily forward with a long silver claw.

Vampire fangs appeared at the edge of her thin lips as the Sorceress embraced Emily, pulling her into darkness—

"Emily, are you in there?"

Emily opened her eyes to find two noses, one furry, one damp and cool, in her face.

Dreamer gave her a lick as Ozzie dropped a tangle of curly hair back over her face. Wiping sleepy eyes, Emily let the nightmare fade.

"We brought you something to eat," Adriane said, standing by the bunk bed. She handed Emily a covered tray and a container of juice.

Suddenly feeling famished, Emily swung her legs to the wooden floor and opened the tray. "Thank you," she said, biting into the most delicious tuna sandwich she had ever tasted. "Why didn't you wake me earlier?"

"You were exhausted," Adriane said. "The social butterfly mage covered for you at dinner."

"Hey, kids," Kara said, bounding through the screen door and flouncing on the bed next to Emily. "Veronica invited me to the Moonlite Mudbath at the spa tonight."

"Yeah, great," Emily mumbled over a pickle.

"Look, Emily, I was just trying to be friendly," Kara said. "You should give her a chance."

"Well, thanks for keeping her busy."

"No prob." Kara popped open two matching floral suitcases. Their contents immediately spilled out. She started sorting through shoes, pastel bandanas, silk shirts, jackets, and assorted outfits.

Emily pulled her hair back, taming it with a scrunchy.

"Can you still hear them?" Ozzie asked, ferret face full of concern.

"Not now."

"Ozzie filled us in," Adriane explained. "Dreamer and I checked the grounds. No sign of unusual whirlwinds or any magical activity. We think it was isolated to that canyon, drawn to the magic of whatever's in the caves."

Emily nodded.

Kara was neatly laying out several outfits. "Well, you can go out tomorrow morning and look around all you want."

"No," Emily said. "We have to go *now!*"

Kara put her hands on her hips. "You're going to go wandering around in the desert *now?*"

"We can't wait," Emily said, slipping into her hiking boots. "Whatever animals are in there could be hurt."

"Emily says we go, we go!" Adriane said.

Dreamer paced the room and sent an image of the moon.

"Come on, you can say it," Adriane urged.

"The wolf hunts at night."

"That settles it," she said, looking to Kara. "Four against one."

"I'm not going to miss the mudbath to go wandering around in the dirt!" Kara glared, and her hair stuck out like a porcupine.

"Nice," Adriane commented.

"It's at least three miles. How are we going to get there?" Emily asked.

"The Bride of Frankenstein here was kind enough to secure us a ride." Adriane pointed through the screen door. A shiny new golf cart sat in front of the cabin. FOUR WINDS RESORT was stenciled on the sides in looping turquoise.

"No way! I'm not walking, like, way over there." Kara headed to the cabin's bathroom and yelped when she saw her hair in the mirror.

Dreamer huffed, the equivalent of a mistwolf laugh.

With a brilliant zap, Kara tamed her hair back to normal. Satisfied, she cleared Emily and Adriane's toothbrushes off the shelf and started carefully arranging her lipstick from palest to darkest pink. "Maybe I'll just keep it like Veronica's." As Kara spoke, her blond tresses twisted and shimmered into Veronica's flowing black mane.

"Don't do that!" Emily said angrily.

Kara gulped and shut her eyes in concentration. Her hair turned blond. "Sorry."

Emily paused on the woven Southwestern rug. "It's not funny."

"It's not a fashion accessory. Get your jewel under control!" Adriane ordered.

Kara fretted, twisting the unicorn jewel in her hand. "I am, I'm trying . . ."

Emily saw a glint of fear in Kara's eyes. "Okay, you stay here, Kara," she said, plucking the jean jacket from her suitcase.

"Let's move out," Adriane ordered, zipping her down vest. "Anything happens, you call us right away," she said to Kara.

"Check." Kara saluted.

Adriane, Dreamer, Emily, and Ozzie barreled out the cabin's screen door.

"Your carriage, m'lady." Adriane bowed formally, gesturing to the golf cart.

"Thank you, kind knave," Emily giggled, stepping into the front passenger seat. Dreamer and Ozzie climbed in back.

Adriane swung into the driver's seat and started the ignition, Dreamer and Ozzie hanging anxiously over her shoulder.

"Hey, no sweat, I've been driving lawn mowers since I was seven."

The cart jumped backward.

"Okay, eight." The cart lurched forward, crunching along the gravel-covered path that wound between clusters of cabins.

"The trail starts beyond that big rock," Emily pointed.

Adriane swung the cart off the main road, jostling over small rocks and brush.

The last golden glow of sunset had disappeared, swallowing the desert in darkness. Adriane switched the headlights on, projecting a bright circle of light. They rode in open desert for thirty minutes, Emily and Ozzie directing them by landmarks spotted earlier that day.

"There's Echo Ridge," Emily said, pointing to a shadowy wall looming in the distance. "Follow the ridgeline east." She moved her finger. "The canyon's about a mile . . . over there."

Adriane steered the cart toward the canyon. The rising moon cast its ghostly white glow over the land, making everything stand out in stark relief.

At the wide entrance to the canyon, Adriane brought the cart to a stop.

Mages, Ozzie, and Dreamer sat listening to the night sounds of the desert. Insects chirped and buzzed, a coyote brayed in the distance.

"There's a big cave on the far side of the canyon," Ozzie said.

The warrior looked at her jewel. It lay quietly on her wrist.

Dreamer raised his nose in the air and sniffed. With a bark, he leaped from the cart.

"What you got?" Adriane asked.

"Magic."

"Okay, but stay close."

With Dreamer leading the way, eagerly sniffing the night air, Adriane drove the cart into the canyon.

"Mage?"

A soft voice crept into Emily's head.

"Yes, I'm here."

"Are you really a mage?"

"Yes."

"Then what's my name? Quiet, Clio! Don't speak to strangers!"

"Clio," Emily answered.

"Ooo, you hear that, Riannan? She heard me say that, you bubblebrain!"

"Another message?" Adriane asked, sensing Emily's thoughts.

"Yes, let's hurry."

Emily's jumbled thoughts settled on the memory of a beautiful white unicorn.

Lorelei was her name. The Dark Sorceress had captured Lorelei and cut her horn off in an effort to steal the unicorn's magic. Emily shuddered, not wanting to think about what they were going to find. It was her job to feel that pain and heal it.

"Emily!" Adriane whispered, holding up her wolf stone. It blazed with a warning golden light.

The healer's hazel eyes shone, reflecting the deep green light of her pulsing rainbow gem.

"Where's it coming from?" Ozzie looked all around, his stone also ablaze with a magical warning.

Dreamer sent an image of sand.

Adriane held out her arm, focusing a beam of light across the surrounding sands. Nothing moved in the silvery desert dreamscape. "I don't see anything."

The mistwolf's hackles rose, and he whirled around, growling.

The golf cart suddenly rose and lowered as if cresting a wave.

"Whoa!" Ozzie called out, "Look!"

Behind them, the desert floor billowed and rolled like a stormy sea.

Emily held on tight, then stood, her jewel radiating light. The threat was all around them. "Faster, Adriane!"

"We're going as fast as we can!" Her foot was flat against the cart's front plate.

"I think I see—"

Emily landed on the ground, face first in sand. She twisted around and looked up. The cart careened into the air. Spinning head over wheels, it landed with a blunt thud.

Pushing to her knees, she frantically looked for Adriane.

The blaze of golden light caught Emily's eye as she saw the warrior whipping circles of fire from her wolf stone.

"Emily! Are you all right?"

"I think so." She tried to clear her head and squinted. The sands swelled with movement. Something was *swimming* in there. Something dangerous. A sharp fin rose, slicing its way toward her. She couldn't outrun it, it was too fast.

A monster erupted from the sands not three feet in front of her! For an instant, Emily saw its massive sharklike head and maw of stalactite teeth.

Dreamer crashed headfirst into it, viciously ripping at the thing's throat

The shark twisted and leaped, its full body rising out of the desert sand.

Adriane aimed her wolf stone, and golden fire flew in the night, striking fast and hard. The beast exploded in a cloud of sand and stone.

"It's made of sand!" Emily shielded her eyes from falling debris.

Adriane cut the stream of magic, sharply pulling the fire back to her wrist.

Behind the dust, flashing lights suddenly appeared in the desert sky.

"Spaceships!" Ozzie yelled.

A whirlwind spun into existence. Bright reds, greens, and purples cast an eerie glow across the sand.

"Another magic whirlwind!" Emily cried.

Like a snake, the whirlwind burrowed into the ground. Amid the roiling desert, eight sharp fins materialized.

"Where's the cave, Ozzie?" Emily shouted.

"Er . . . this way . . . no over there . . . *Gah!*"

A huge dorsal fin burst from the sand, sending the ferret skidding to a stop.

"Dreamer! Cover our backs!" Adriane ordered, honing the glowing golden beam from her gem into a light saber. "Emily, take the right! Ozzie, the left!"

"We can't hold them, Adriane," Emily cried. "Run!"

But it was too late. Sharklike fins dove in and out of the sands, circling them. The mages were completely surrounded.

Chapter 6

The desert churned as the creatures swarmed, sending rippling waves of sand against the four defenders of magic. Emily, Adriane, Ozzie, and Dreamer stood back-to-back, gems drawn. The mistwolf bared his teeth, growling low and dangerously.

"Steady, stay sharp," Adriane said, wielding her sword of wolf light.

"Look out!" Ozzie screamed.

Sand erupted as an enormous beast attacked. Its huge body surged from the desert, long teeth gnashing.

Adriane sliced the beast in half, sending sand raining everywhere. Dreamer tried to block another sand shark, but he accidentally barreled into Adriane's legs, almost knocking her over.

"Dreamer, stay behind me!" the warrior ordered.

The second beast lunged. Silvery moonlight reflected off crystal teeth as the creature's gaping maw stretched wide. Adriane fired a bolt of fire down its throat, exploding the thing into a cloud of sand.

Several more creatures came at the group from all sides.

"There's too many!" Ozzie smacked his ferret stone, trying to make it do something.

A shadow swirled across the ground as a dark shape swooped from the sky.

"Incoming!" Ozzie cried.

With a fierce growl, the flying creature dove right into the attacking monsters, razor claws flashing. The beasts were ripped to bits of sand and rocks in a matter of seconds.

"Lyra!" Emily cried.

"The way is open, run!" the flying cat called.

"Go, go, go!" Adriane yelled. She leaped and spun, lashing a stream of golden wolf light at another beast.

Dreamer barked and growled.

Another whirlwind materialized, this one much smaller. Adriane landed in a fighting stance, ready to unleash her fire.

"Adriane, wait," Emily yelled.

Veering crazily, the tiny whirlwind wobbled to a stop, revealing a small, twiggy figure.

"Tweek!" Emily cried.

"The magic's gone wild!" the E.F. squeaked, quartz eyes spinning in his head. "Took me forever to get . . ."—he found himself eye to quartz with another sand shark—"baaaaaaack!"

The shark swallowed Tweek whole.

Adriane lassoed her golden light into a fiery rope and closed it around the thrashing beast.

The little twig figure freed, fell to the ground in a cloud of sand. "Fascinating! This elemental magic is like nothing I've seen before."

The desert rumbled ominously.

"Everyone into the cave!" Adriane ordered, herding the group across the remaining distance.

Stumbling over the undulating sands, Ozzie grabbed the E.F.

They entered the dark cave. The mage's jewels wove gold and blue light across the interior, illuminating an immense chamber.

Lyra landed inside, and Emily ran to hug the big cat.

"I am *soo* happy to see you!" she cried.

Lyra nuzzled her sleek head against Emily's face, her bright green cat's eyes dancing. *"I couldn't let you go on an adventure without me."*

Adriane scratched behind Lyra's ears. "Would never be the same. How did you ever find us?"

"I just looked for magical mayhem," Lyra purred playfully as Adriane rubbed the cat's neck. *"Of course, I was expecting to find the blazing star."*

Staring into the black depths of the cavern, Tweek, still in Ozzie's grip, spoke quietly: "Adventure? Is this a normal day for you mages?"

"Tweek, this is Adriane, Dreamer, and Lyra." Emily introduced her friends.

"Pleased to meet you. I'm an experimen-*geek*!"

"Yeah, we know," Ozzie said, shaking a few loose branches from the E.F. "Why do you always show up when something bad is happening?"

"Ozzie!" Emily scolded. "Put him down."

"It's not my fault," Tweek said, losing a few stray twigs and scrub. "Someone is using fairy magic to twist elements of nature."

"Who?" Ozzie asked, arms crossed over his chest.

"I don't know. Only Fairimentals are supposed to use elemental magic."

"I knew that," Ozzie replied.

"Someone is after the lost magic," Emily guessed.

"Yes, yes!" Tweek waved his twiggy arms.

HOoooo! Teeeeooo! SQuooooK!

Mournful sounds echoed from the depths of the dank cave.

"What was that?" Tweek asked.

Emily stood as still as a statue. The noises

pulsed in a rhythm strangely familiar to her. "I think that's your missing magic—unicorns."

"Unicorns? Tweek gasped. "Sounds awful!"

Adriane spread her golden light across the back walls, revealing a series of tunnels running in several directions. "Which tunnel leads us to the magic, Dreamer?"

More strange out-of-tune noises echoed through the cave.

Dreamer barked excitedly, pointing his nose to the tunnel on the far right.

"Lead the way," Adriane told her pack mate.

The tunnel snaked through honeycombed caverns, the mages' magic gems illuminating eerie limestone fingers on either side. It was if they had wandered into a subterranean universe. They passed extraordinary natural sculptures that looked like frozen waterfalls and melted castles. Along the ground, weird lacy rocks twisted crazily and disappeared into the dark. Emily could sense they were going deep underground.

TOOT! BLAARP! LAA!

"That way." Emily pointed as the tunnel ended in several other offshoots. She edged in front of Dreamer, moving quickly. The noises were getting more agitated.

"It's getting stronger," Emily said.

Dreamer agreed, growling low in his throat.

"Be careful." Ozzie walked in front of Emily protectively, his stone emitting a faint golden glow.

They passed a huge chamber. Enormous stalactites hung like icicles from the ceiling. Trails of iridescent water dripped along their ghostly lengths and onto spiky, yellowish stalagmite spires surging from the cavern floor.

"It's got to be right around here!" Emily said, continuing down the tunnel, her stone now pulsing bright blue.

"I don't see anythi—*agHp*!"

TWONK!

Ozzie bounced off . . . nothing!

"Ozzie, are you all right?"

"Perfect!" The ferret leaped to his feet, whiskers springing back in place.

Reaching over the ferret, Emily's fingers bumped up against an invisible barrier. "There's something here," she said, running her blue and lavender jewel light over the area. Wherever the light hit, a shimmering silver shield was revealed.

"A protection shield!" Tweek said excitedly "Ooo, Gwigg was right, you are good!"

"They're in there," Emily whispered. Placing both hands against the shield, she leaned in close. "Can you hear me?"

Go away! Leave us alone, you snarkmoose! There's no one in here! Shhhhh!

"We're not going to hurt you," Emily said, trying to send calming vibes through the barrier. She looked to Adriane and nodded.

The black-haired mage summoned a thread of golden magic and directed it carefully at the shield. It bounced off, ricocheting over Tweek's head.

"Now what?" the warrior asked.

"The HORARFF!" Tweek exclaimed.

"Bless you." Ozzie patted the E.F. on the back

"No, no, the HORARFF: *Handbook of Rules and Regulations for Fairimentals!*" Tweek held the little turquoise gemstone at his neck. "This might tell us how to get past the shield."

Tweek's quartz eyes sparked in concentration, and a glowing orb blossomed from the gem. Strange symbols and images flashed rapidly through the little sphere, casting shifting shadows upon the rocky walls of the cavern.

"It's like a fairy map!" Adriane exclaimed.

"Something like that," Tweek said, studying the symbols.

"The HORARFF is tuned to me, so I'm the only one who can operate it," Tweek explained. "Ah, here we go. This barrier is a unicorn shield. The only way to get through it is to use unicorn magic. I don't suppose anyone has some lying around?"

"We don't, but—" Emily started.

"We know someone who does," Adriane finished.

"You'd better call her, Lyra," Emily said to the cat.

Lyra nodded.

"Who, who?" Tweek asked excitedly "Another mage?"

"The pink one," Adriane answered dryly.

"Tell her to get the dragonflies to open a portal," Emily continued. "It's the only way to get her here. We took her golf cart."

The cat closed her green eyes to send the message telepathically to Kara. Lyra's face scrunched, and her brow furrowed as if she was arguing.

"Wait!" Tweek exclaimed, jumping excitedly. "The blazing star, right?"

"Bingo," Adriane muttered.

Lyra opened her eyes and grimaced. *She's not happy, but she's coming.*

Pop! POP! Pop! POP! Pop!

Suddenly, bubbles of bright light like starbursts popped into the cave, each bearing a brilliantly colored flying mini dragon.

"Dee Dee! Emeee!"

Purple Barney, red Fiona, blue Fred, orange

Blaze, and yellow Goldie flew about the mages excitedly.

"*Ozooo!*" Barney flopped onto Ozzie's head.

"Gah! Get off me, you pest!"

"Hi guys," Emily said, scratching Fiona under her little neck.

The dragonflies immediately brushed against the shield, cooing and oohing.

"Yes, we need to get in there, but we need Kara."

"*Oooo!*"

The five minis hooked wingtips together and formed a circle, spinning and whirring, creating a swirling mass of color. They were forming a portal.

The tunnel walls rumbled and shook as if a train had passed underneath.

"I don't like the feel of that," Adriane said, glancing at her wolf stone.

"You think whatever attacked us outside has followed us in?" Emily asked worriedly.

Tweek's quartz eyes started spinning. "Something awful is coming!"

"*Kee kee!*" Goldie squeaked.

In a burst of diamond light, a figure stepped from the portal's center and into the cave.

"AHHH!" Tweek screamed, barreling into Ozzie as he tried to flee, twigs and sticks flying.

Kara scowled, cracking the thick brown mud mask plastered to her face. Her plush white terrycloth robe and matching towel turban only made the brown mask stand out more.

"Try not to let her beauty blind you," Adriane cracked to Tweek.

"This better be good!" the blazing star fumed.

"We found the source of magic, but it's behind a shield," Emily explained, pressing her hand against the barrier. "Tweek says we need your unicorn jewel to get past it."

"I can't!" Kara said adamantly.

"What do you mean you can't?" Adriane asked. "Your jewel is the only thing that can open it."

"Kara, what's wrong?" Emily asked, sensing the dread in Kara's words.

"I . . . well . . . you know . . ." Kara twirled the belt of her robe with trembling fingers and looked away.

The mages stared at her.

"My magic is all *flooie*!" she burst out.

"Flooie . . ." Tweek quickly began looking up "flooie" in his brightly glowing jewel.

"Would you turn that off? It's blinding me!" Ozzie yelled at the E.F..

"Kara, we know you've had some problems with your jewel," Emily said gently.

"I'll say! I turned the mudbath into Jell-O!"

"We'll help you, okay?" Emily said soothingly. "Trust us."

Kara looked at the faces of her friends. "Fine," she said, holding up her unicorn jewel. "But if I change you into a brimbee, I'll blame you."

Adriane and Emily stood on either side of Kara holding up their jewel.

Kara stretched her arms wide. "Do you mind?" she asked the pile of twigs at her feet.

The E.F. moved away to give her some room.

Kara gingerly raised her unicorn jewel. "Okay, let's do this—my mud is caking."

Emily and Adriane touched Kara's hands. Shaking, Kara pointed her jewel at the shield.

Sparkling magic spilled from the gem, completely surrounding her. Only it didn't have the desired effect. With a brilliant burst, her robe sprouted into a hairy red pelt!!

"Does it come in black?" Adriane asked.

Kara's face flushed.

"Try again," Emily encouraged.

Unsteadily, Kara released another blast.

"Your face!" Adriane clapped her hand over her mouth.

This time, a rainbow of feathers had sprouted from Kara's mud mask.

"Fantastic!" Tweek exclaimed.

Adriane and Emily touched Kara's hands, sending gold and blue light spiraling up and around the blazing star. Scowling with frustration,

Kara tried one last time. Crystalline light beamed forth, melting the invisible barrier. The shield glowed, then shrunk into a small, flat silver object that plopped into Kara's hand.

"Hey, cool, a protection amulet—I was reading about these," she said.

But no one was paying attention to Kara. The blond girl turned around to see what everyone was staring at.

Thirty pairs of wide eyes looked back in silent terror.

Chapter 7

"**O**ooooo, ponies!" Kara squealed.

A herd of beige and white creatures with lanky legs and flowing manes trembled against the cave wall.

Tweek hopped up and down, loose twigs flying. "Those aren't ponies, those are unicorns!"

Help, it's a fuzzy muckle! EeoooPP! No, it's a werebird! FhoooB!

WWAAAAAAAAHHHHHHHHH!

The terrified unicorns burst into tears, pushing and stumbling over one another to get as far away from Kara as possible.

Wild unicorn magic erupted uncontrolled. The cave shuddered as fireworks sparked across the ceiling. Stalactites shattered, sending jagged shards flying.

"Keee KEEaaaaa!!!"

The frightened dragonflies dodged falling rocks and disappeared in bursts of brilliant bubbles. The unicorns wailed louder.

Help!!! OOOaaaaHHHHH!

Rainbow arcs of unfocused power swirled and flashed. A huge stalactite plummeted and crashed to the floor.

"HowwUUUU!!" Dreamer howled, racing about in circles as the wild magic pummeled his senses.

WWWAAAAAAHHHHH!

Diamond light streamed from Kara's unicorn jewel, forcing her backward. The magic swung over the unicorns' heads, slamming into the walls. "I can't control my jewel!" she screamed.

Lyra roared, leaping to Kara's side to keep her from falling. Ozzie frantically waved his paws.

Emily had never felt such strong magic. The panic and pain of these creatures crashed into her senses, wild and raw. Falling to her knees, she fought to keep from fainting as the room spun around her.

"Help me, Ozzie," she gasped.

"Emily!" Ozzie cried, his ferret stone exploding in bright amber light. *"Stop* it!" he yelled to the unicorns. Amplified by his jewel, his voice thundered over the chaos. "You're hurting her!"

The unicorns looked up, startled into silence. Their magic faded.

"Thank you," Emily said, catching her breath.

Adriane ran to Emily's side, helping her up.

"Easy," the warrior said.

Fighting past the unicorns' fear, Emily reached into the calm, bright center of her healing powers.

"It's okay," she said, sending a shimmering wave of blue-green magic over the terrified creatures. "We're not going to hurt you."

The unicorns looked wonderingly at the red-haired girl.

"What about the fuzzy muckle?" a unicorn sniffled.

"I am not a fuzzy muckle!" Kara scraped at her plumed mud mask and took the towel turban off her head. Her blond hair sprang up in long spikes.

The unicorns looked at one another, squeaking like out-of-tune bagpipes.

"I'm Emily," she said softly. "I heard you calling to me."

Tweek walked among the lanky legs, counting. ". . . twenty-eight . . . -nine . . . thirty. . . . It's the entire class of unicorn trainees!"

"But where are their horns?" Kara asked.

"Their horns haven't grown yet, thank goodness," Tweek explained. "They're babies."

Am not! I'm almost one!

"How'd you get here?" Emily asked the little unicorns.

SQEeeOONK!! TOOT! . . . couldn't find the portal and . . . BEEP! SQUooooK! . . . we fell over the bridge . . . pHloop . . . I bumped my head!

All the unicorns brayed at once in a combination of screeching sounds and jumbled thoughts. The chaos unleashed bursts of wild magic again.

Emily gasped.

"Gah!" Ozzie yelled, stone pulsing. "One at a time!"

The unicorns turned their heads into a protective huddle. A hoof rose up as one unlucky unicorn was booted from the group. He landed on his rump in front of the mages. He had very large ears, a bulbous nose, and a forelock that stuck straight up. Realizing it was up to him, he took a deep breath and blurted his story.

"My name's Pollo, and we were on our way to Dalriada, but the monsters found us and we must have fallen through a portal and landed here. Then we ran into this cave and used the amulet shield to hide us."

Honk!

Another baby unicorn, taller than the others, with a beautiful flowing mane and tail, peeked out. Realizing Pollo wasn't going to get eaten, she pushed him out of the way and took over. *"How'd you get past the shield?"*

"This is Kara," Emily explained, pointing to the blazing star. "Her unicorn jewel opened it."

Oooo! All the unicorns looked at the sparkling jewel dangling between Kara's fingers.

"I demand you take us out of here," the tall unicorn said adamantly.

"*Riannan, it really is a unicorn jewel!*" Pollo said.

What!? The unicorns looked at one another.

"*Who are you?*" Riannan demanded.

"*I'm your brother, Pollo.*"

"*Not you!*" Riannan stamped a sparkly hoof. "*You!*"

"This is Adriane, Lyra, Dreamer, and Ozzie," Emily said. "We're from Ravenswood."

"*Just because they say they are doesn't mean anything,*" Riannan sniffed, swatting her golden tail against Pollo's skinny flank. "*Everyone stay back.*"

The unicorns all pushed past Riannan to examine the girls and magical animals.

"Hey, you know I rode a big unicorn," Kara said with a brilliant smile.

She's a blazing star! Wowhoot!

The babies piled around her.

"May I see that?" Tweek asked Kara, reaching for the protection amulet in her hand.

She handed the amulet to the twiggy guy.

Tweek ran a beam of light from his own jewel over the silvery object. "This is a very powerful amulet. And it's been tuned to the unicorn jewel. Someone sent the unicorns to you."

"Here?" Adriane asked, incredulously.

"*Gah!*" Ozzie hopped with surprise as a unicorn butted him. The baby's sleek hide was covered with polka-dot spots.

"*I'm Ralfondiz. What are you?*"

"Watch it, Ralfie," the ferret answered.

"Ozzie's another mage," Emily explained. "He's an elf."

"*Are all elves as fuzzy as you?*" Ralfie asked, cocking his head.

"No, I'm extra fuzzy!"

"*I'm Snowflake. Are you a mistwolf?*" A snow-white unicorn asked Dreamer shyly.

"*Big mistwolf,*" Dreamer huffed.

"*I'm Calliope.*" A beige unicorn with big blue eyes sidled up to Kara. The creature's hide twinkled as if coated with fairy dust. "*My hair is all dirty.*" She hung her head.

Kara ran her fingers through Calliope's tangled silky mane. "Not to worry; a little herbal conditioner and you'll look amazing!"

The unicorn beamed.

"*Thank goodness we're rescued!*" another unicorn exclaimed, tripping over her big feet and falling on Lyra. "*Hi. I'm Electra.*"

"*Easy there, Electra.*" Lyra nudged the lanky unicorn to her feet.

An ominous noise rumbled through the cave, dropping bits of rock and dust.

A little unicorn whimpered against Emily. *"Are the monsters still after us?"*

"Violet, you're such a worry wommel," Riannan said, rolling her beautiful dark eyes.

Adriane moved to the cave opening, her wolf stone glowing, warning of imminent danger.

"What attacked you, Violet?" Emily asked.

Violet squeaked and hid her head between her long front legs.

"Big monsters made out of mist," a unicorn with a sock marking on each foot told her.

"I saw better than you, Clio!" another one scoffed. He had a pale blaze on his forehead. *"They were mist monsters."*

"That's what I just said, Dante!" Clio stamped her hooves.

"Whoever made those creatures has powerful conjuring skills!" Tweek exclaimed. "Only a magic master could use fairy magic like that."

"We have to leave this place now," Adriane said decisively.

"Just get us to our wagon and take us to Dalri-ada," Riannan ordered.

"I'm afraid the wagon is gone," Emily said, understanding now how they came here.

"Well, now what do we do?" Riannan groaned.

A howl of rushing wind echoed eerily in the cavern.

BLEEEEEEAAAAAHHHH!

Everyone jumped as a little unicorn blasted a noise like an air horn.

"Spruce, can that honker!" Dante scolded.

"Something bad is coming!" Spruce said, shivering.

A wet, slithering sound echoed down the tunnel.

"Of course, a very powerful fairy creature could be using elemental magic. There are some from the Otherworlds capable of it," Tweek mused.

"How do we fight it?" Adriane asked, looking over her shoulder, down the dark tunnel.

"Fight it? That's quite impossible. You're only Level One mages."

Kara, Adriane, and Emily stared at him.

"I thought we were full mages," Adriane said slowly.

"How many levels are there?" Emily asked.

"Didn't you guys read your HORARFM?" Tweek sighed with exasperation. *"Handbook of Rules and Regulations for Mages!* Your mentor should have given you that."

"We don't have a mentor," Adriane said.

"What?!" Tweek shuddered, losing more twigs. "You mean to tell me you've been wandering around with magic jewels all by yourselves?"

"Hey, what am I?" Ozzie interjected. "Chopped-liver snaps?"

An eerie metallic swishing whispered up the tunnel, getting closer.

Dreamer growled, his hackles standing straight up.

"You won't leave us, will you, Emily?" Violet asked, trembling against the healer's side

"Of course not," Emily said as the unicorns huddled against her and Kara.

"Can't the unicorns open a portal, Tweek?" Kara asked.

"Absolutely not! Their magic is completely unreliable."

"Kara, call the dragonflies back," Adriane said, glancing into the inky tunnel. "Get them to open a portal and we'll go through it, take the unicorns with us."

"Where?" Ozzie asked. "I think Texas Slimbob might notice thirty extra equines hanging around the ranch."

"The empty stalls by the feed room in the barn," Emily suggested. "No one will see us there this time of night."

"Twighead," Ozzie handed the E.F. a branch. "Get the protection shield back up."

"I'm afraid I can't. It has to be recharged,"

Tweek said, looking over the object in his twiggy hand.

"We have our own protection shield," Adriane said, turning to the mistwolf. "Dreamer, turn to mist and cover the cave opening."

The young mistwolf shuffled back and forth, unsure about how to use his special magical abilities.

"You can do it," Adriane ran her hand over the wolf's thick black fur. "Just like we practiced."

"Okay, Kara, let's do it. Hurry!" Emily ordered.

"Oh, all right." The blazing star closed her eyes and called for her mini friends. "Hey! D'flies! Front and center!"

Colored bubbles popped over surprised unicorn faces as a quintet of mini dragonheads carefully peered out.

"*Oooooo.*" Goldie surveyed the situation.

"Goldie, open a portal back to the ranch," Kara ordered. "Get us in the barn."

"*Okeee-dokeee.*"

Squeaking industriously, the pint-sized dragons locked wingtips in circular formation and created a shimmering portal.

Dreamer stood, eyes squeezed tight. His body began to shimmer, and his head suddenly disappeared into a swirl of hazy smoke.

"Concentrate," Adriane urged. "Let the magic run through your body."

Dreamer's head reappeared—but his legs had vanished. The pup whined.

A high-pitched scream filled the tunnel as the slithering sound came closer.

The minis had spun open their portal and were stretching it wide.

"Okay, that's enough. Lemme see." Kara stuck her head through, then stepped back. "We're good to go. Move it, everybody!"

I'm not going first! No way! I hate portals! I threw up!

"Listen up!" Ozzie marched back and forth in front of the little unicorns. "The sooner everyone goes through, the sooner we'll be in a safe barn filled with hay, oats, grain, carrots—"

"Blech, we're not horses, Fuzzy!" Ralfie stuck out his tongue.

"Ozzie. All right, all right, whatever you want to eat, I'll get it *personally*." Ozzie started pushing Ralfie toward the portal. "Now, who's first?"

Dreamer had managed to spread his misty body over the cave opening. His head floated in the center, wide eyes looking none too pleased.

"Not bad," Adriane said. Tight circles of golden fire spun around her wrist and up her arm.

Something huge skittered by the opening. Through the mist, a long body snaked past them.

"*Ahh-!*"

"*Shhhh!*" Riannan swished her tail in Clio's mouth.

"*Ooooooooo.*" The dragonflies were shaking as the portal quivered in and out.

"Go! Someone go first!" Emily hissed.

Without warning a giant creature punched through the mist. Multiple eyes looked everywhere from stalks reaching out of a bulbous head covered with needles. The color of bruised purple, the grotesque centipede creature advanced on dozens of noisily scissoring legs. Thick, oily armor plated its huge body, needles protruding everywhere. Tentacles twitched as its mouth stretched wide in a fetid hiss, revealing rows of sharp, needle teeth.

The unicorns stampeded. Six babies tried to jam themselves through the portal at once. The dragonflies yelped, squashed by the struggling mass.

Lemme through! SPLLARRP! Ow! My nose!

Emily and Ozzie pried the babies apart and pushed them through one by one.

"Keep that portal open, no matter what!" Emily instructed the dragonflies.

Lyra roared, protecting the portal with her shimmering wings.

Adriane was already in motion, whipping a ring of golden wolf light at the monster. Squealing like a ferocious pig, the thing convulsed, armor rattling. Gooey tentacles writhed as the warrior danced out of reach from their twitching grasp.

Kara stepped forward, pointing her glowing unicorn jewel at the creature. A flare of white light shot straight up, slamming the cave ceiling. The blond girl stumbled back, face flushed.

Shrieking, the creature lunged, trying to swallow the unicorns whole.

Adriane struck again, wolf fire hammering the monster's head, forcing its snapping jaws away from the portal.

"Lyra, get everyone through!" Adriane yelled. "We're right behind you. Move!"

Ozzie and Tweek crammed the last two frightened unicorns through the portal and raced in. Nosing Kara and Emily through, Lyra leaped and disappeared.

"Dreamer, go!" Adriane looked around frantically. "Where are you?"

"Pack mate! Go!"

Dreamer stood in solid wolf form right in front of the monster.

The thing swung its massive head, mouth gaping.

Moving with lightning speed, Adriane raced past the creature and shoved Dreamer into the portal. The dragonflies squealed as the warrior dove through.

Shrieking, the monster charged in after them.

Chapter 8

Adriane and Dreamer tumbled onto the barn's floor, the monster's foul breath hot on their backs.

Needle teeth gnashing, the creature thrashed its head through the portal.

The warrior rolled into a fighting stance, crossing her wrists in front of her face. "Dreamer, behind me!" she commanded as wolf light surged from her jewel.

GrEEP! Hide me! Snoooop! Run away!

The unicorns scrambled through the barn, diving into stalls. Horses neighed, surprised at their visitors as Lyra nosed the stragglers out of harm's way.

Adriane swung her wolf stone, releasing a fury of magic.

With a fierce growl, Dreamer leaped at the monster—right in the path of the bolt.

"No!" Adriane wrenched her jewel away. Light

arced wildly, wrapping the warrior in sparking golden fire.

The monster lunged, closing its massive jaws completely around Dreamer.

ZZZZAP!

In a brilliant flash, the portal vanished, severing the gruesome head. Slime-covered skin and twisting eyes morphed into a pile of green guck that splattered to the floor. Unharmed, Dreamer shook drops of goo from his fur.

Five dragonflies peered from a floating bubble. *"Kaakaa!"*

"Good job, D'flies!" Kara called out.

"Get off me, Ralfie!" Dante complained, crawling out of a stall.

"Where are we?" Ralfie asked, bits of hay stuck to his forelock.

"It's okay, you're safe now," Emily said, sending a wave of calming magic over the frightened horses. She shut the barn door before Electra could stumble outside.

Ozzie ran about, herding the babies to the stalls.

Adriane picked sticky muck out of Dreamer's fur. "You have to learn to listen to me! Next time we won't be so lucky!"

Dreamer's eyes were downcast.

Gently, Adriane raised Dreamer's head, looking deep into his emerald eyes.

"Pack mate."

"Yes." Adriane hugged the wolf close. "What would I do if I lost you?"

"Looks like my grandma's creamed spinach." Kara wrinkled her nose at the gob of goo splattered across the floor. "What *was* that thing?"

"Elemental, my dear mage." Tweek plucked something from the guck. "A prickly pear needle, I believe."

"So it was what, a cactipede?" Kara asked.

"All this magic isn't supposed to be on Earth," Tweek fretted, wringing his crackling twig hands as he looked at the unicorns.

"We have to get to Dalriada," Riannan said, stamping her feet.

The others squeaked and tooted like a broken carousel.

"Okay, everyone settle down," Emily said, herding Snowflake and Pollo into the stall. "You have to stay here until we can figure out what to do."

"If that elemental magic found them in the desert, it will find them here," Adriane pointed out. "The unicorns are sitting ducks without the protection shield."

"What's a duck?" Electra asked, flopping over a hay bale.

"How do we recharge the amulet, Tweek?" Emily asked.

"You'd need real unicorn magic," Tweek said.

PhoOOT!

"But that's out of the question," the E.F. continued. "Without their horns, there's no way for them to focus their magic. It'll just go wild like it did in the cave."

"What if *we* could focus the unicorns' magic?" Emily asked.

Tweek eyed her suspiciously. "How would you do that?"

"You said it was tuned to Kara's unicorn jewel," Emily said. "Maybe we can help the unicorns."

"That might work—" Tweek began.

"Nuh-uh." Kara closed her hand around her jewel and sighed. "Okay, you guys, I admit it, I don't know what I'm doing with it."

"We'll help you, Kara," Emily pressed.

The unicorns sat up listening.

"It's worth a shot," Adriane said.

"Let's all form a circle," Emily instructed.

Scuffling and bumping into one another, the babies managed to form a ring in the center of the barn. Ozzie marched around, pushing or pulling a unicorn here and there to make the circle even. Tweek stood in the center holding the amulet containing the shield in his twig. "This is highly irregular."

Radiant gold arced from Adriane's wolf stone, surrounding the amulet. Summoning a dazzling beam of pure blue, Emily's healing magic swirled around the warrior's.

Holding out her gem and pointing it at the amulet, Kara shut her eyes. Blazing white magic exploded from the unicorn jewel, engulfing Emily's and Adriane's steady light.

Kara shrieked—her hand had morphed into a giant hairy goblin hand!

Ewww! That's gross!

The blond girl coiled huge stubby fingers around her jewel, her face tense with determination. In a flash she had her hand back, with a bonus: freshly polished pink nails.

"The unicorn jewel is completely flooie," Tweek announced.

"Unicorns can use music to focus magic," Emily said excitedly to her friends, remembering she had helped heal Lorelei with a special song.

"Spellsinging," Kara finished Emily's train of thought.

"That's strong fairy magic," Tweek said, astonished. "How do you know about— Never mind, I don't want to know."

Emily faced the herd. "I'll hum a note, and you follow. Ready?"

Yay! Oooo, fun! Me, me, me first!

"This is silly! I'm not singing!" Riannan stamped her hoof down.

"Riannan's a 'fraidy corn!" one of the others teased.

"Am not!" she shot back.

Emily pressed her lips together and hummed a single pure note.

A deafening racket of blaring noise rattled the barn.

"Stop!" Ozzie yelled.

BlaaRp?

Emily smiled. "You have to follow the music. Let it flow." Remembering the beautiful song she and Lorelei had sung together, she hummed the first verse. Pollo's little squawk joined her, wavering an octave too high, but in tune.

"Good. Now you try it." Emily nodded toward another.

"WEEEEAHHHHHHHH!" Spruce blasted in an abrasive tenor.

"Concentrate on singing together," Emily told the unicorns. "Listen to everybody around you."

Clio and Snowflake started tooting.

Violet added a soft, shaky note.

"That's nice, Violet," Emily said.

"Easy there, guys," Kara said nervously, watching her jewel pulse with light.

Dante, Electra, and Ralfie tootled and honked. Not to be outdone, Calliope joined in with a bell-like tinkling. Soon every unicorn jingled, jangled, yodeled, and yelped. Except for Riannan, who stuck her nose in the air and huffed.

Power flared from Kara's jewel, enough to make the amulet pulse radiant silver.

"Look!" Tweek said. "It's working."

"FLEeepBaaarrG." Spruce unleashed a blast of off-key noise.

Dante and Pollo sang louder, each trying to outdo the other.

Calliope tried to drown out the boys.

Kara's magic undulated strong and bright, threatening to burst free of her control. Emily and Adriane twined their streams of magic around Kara's white-hot beam, holding it steady by creating a braid of liquid diamond, amber, and topaz.

In a bright flash, the unicorn amulet projected a small, shimmering bubble hovering in the air.

"Holy HORARFF!" Tweek exclaimed.

Everyone watched as the glowing lines encircled a network of stars. A fiery pulse swept along one line intersecting with a series of shining points.

"You've unlocked a fairy map!" Tweek explained.

"We've seen plenty of those," Kara said, making Tweek jumble. "Each one of those stars is a portal."

"That's where we started from," Pollo said, pointing a hoof at a blinking light at the edge of the map.

"So then," Emily said, following the bright line to a last blinking star, "there is where you have to go, Dalriada."

"Inconceivable!" Tweek blustered, twigs flying. "They can't open a portal without their horns. Besides, with the web all crazy, we can't trust this map to be accurate anymore. Who knows where you'll end up?"

"We'll worry about that later. Right now we need to get the shield over the entire ranch," Adriane said, guiding Kara between herself and Emily.

Dreamer and Lyra stepped closer. The unicorns closed their eyes in concentration.

Emily reached out with her magic. She could *feel* her power coursing through the map. "I add the protection of healer magic," she called out.

Adriane's amber wolf magic pulsed bright. "I add the strength of a warrior!"

Now it was up to Kara. She took a breath and lifted her jewel high. "I add the fire of the blazing star to bind it together!"

The fairy map was replaced by a glittering dome hovering in the air.

"That's it!" Tweek yelled.

The mages stepped back, allowing their magic to stretch the shield wider and wider. It floated to the ceiling in shimmering blue, gold, and white magic, passed through the roof, and vanished.

"I can't believe my quartz—you did it!" Tweek yelled, handling the amulet back to Kara.

"How long's it good for?" Adriane asked.

"Few days, maybe," Tweek said, pacing wildly. "O' me twig!"

Emily plopped down in the hay, exhausted. Clio, Spruce, Violet, Pollo, and Snowflake piled over her, snuggling close.

"We rock!" Ralphie brayed proudly.

"What's Dalriada?" Kara asked, carefully draping a blanket over the hay so she and Calliope could sit without getting dusty.

"That's where the Unicorn Academy is," Calliope responded, nudging the others away from the blazing star.

"I'm going to run the web!" Dante snorted

"I'm going to run it faster!" Ralfie said.

Dante and Ralfie began tussling, rolling over Ozzie.

"GarG!"

"I'm going to run with a blazing star!" Calliope eyed Kara lovingly.

"We have to get these unicorns to Dalriada before their horns sprout." Tweek stumbled over the mages to examine each of the unicorn's foreheads closely.

"What do you mean, Tweek?" Emily asked.

"The first thing they're trained to do is tune magic with their horns. Without proper supervision, it would be disastrous—O' me Twig!" Tweek's quartz eyes began spinning wildly.

"Whoa," Dante went cross-eyed as Tweek stood on the unicorn's nose, brushing away his forelock.

"This is awful, just terrible!" the E.F. wailed.

"What's wrong?" Emily asked.

"Look!" Tweek shuddered uncontrollably, pointing a twig at Dante's head. "His horn is about to sprout!"

"That's right, I'm bad!" Dante proudly displayed a small nub protruding from his forehead.

"OOOOO!!" The unicorns all started concentrating, trying to make their horns sprout.

"AHHH!" Tweek was in a frenzy.

Ozzie grabbed the distraught E.F. "Keep yourself together, man!"

"There're *thirty* unicorns. It's an almost inconceivable amount of power! If they can't control their horns, it could throw the *entire* web off balance!" Tweek cried, shuddering dangerously. "I'm just a rookie!"

BANG! The E.F. burst apart in a huge explosion of twigs.

"Not much for good-byes, is he?" Ozzie commented.

Violet brushed shyly against Emily. *"You can teach us how to tune our horns, Emily."*

"Pleeeezzzzz!" the others pleaded.

"We'll see," Emily said, rubbing her eyes. "But right now we're tired. It's been a long night. Ozzie, I want you to stay here."

"What?" The rest of the ferret's protest was lost as the unicorns nuzzled up to him.

"I'll stay as well," Lyra said.

"We're hungry, Fuzzy," Clio complained, dancing on her socked legs.

"You did say something about feeding them, as I recall," Emily said, smiling.

Food! Food! Food! Food! Yea, FuZZY!

"The name's 'Ozzie'!" the ferret protested. Then, throwing his paws up, the ferret gave in. "Fine, I'll get you some . . . uh . . . what *do* you eat?"

"Unicorn food, what else?" Ralphie laughed, making his spotted coat jiggle.

"Er, remind me again what's in it."

"It's easy," Dante said.

"Pure morning dew," Riannan began, swishing her beautiful tail.

"And a handful of starlight," Spruce honked loudly.

"Don't forget fresh honey!" Electra pushed clumsily to the front of the group.

Licking his lips so enthusiastically he lapped his big round nose, Pollo chimed in: "And you have to stir it exactly nine times under the light of the moon."

Ozzie gaped in disbelief. "How much of this stuff do I have to make?"

"I could eat two whole batches!" Snowflake exclaimed.

The others squawked and tootled in agreement.

Leaving Lyra with Ozzie, the weary mages walked back to their cabin. This day had been like nothing Emily ever could have predicted.

She looked at the star-filled sky and thought about what Tweek had told them. The babies had already attracted strong magic. If their horns sprouted, there might as well be a neon sign over New Mexico advertising thirty baby unicorns.

A simple protection amulet wouldn't do much good, then. And, according to Tweek, the mages' combined Level One powers didn't even have a chance against whatever evil was out there.

Emily had to get these unicorns to safety. Their lives depended on it, and somehow she knew Avalon depended on it, too.

Chapter 9

Glowing golden sunlight crested the horizon over the Happy Trails Horse Ranch. The mages and Dreamer walked quietly but quickly past the cabins. They'd awoken at dawn to check on the unicorns while the rest of the resort was still sleeping.

"So, what's the plan?" Kara asked the healer.

"I don't know, okay?" Emily said, more grouchily than she meant. "I'm sorry. All I know is, we have to get them to the academy before their horns appear."

Adriane agreed. "We'll just have to chance using the fairy map."

"You heard Twighead. Without their horns, they can't open a portal," Kara reminded them.

"Then we're going to need as much unicorn power as we can get," Adriane eyed Kara's gem.

"Don't look at me, I can't even turn my nails pink without making my head green." Kara bit her lip. "What if I have to give it back?" she wailed, clutching her jewel. "Maybe it was a mistake!"

"Kara, the jewel was meant for you," Emily reassured her. "It attracts magic like you do. It just has to be tuned a little differently."

"Absorbing all that fairy magic didn't help, Rapunzel," Adriane commented.

"It's making it worse!" Kara conceded, looking looked at her friends.

"We won't let anything happen to it, or to you," Emily pledged.

"We're in this together—, got it?" Adriane concluded.

"Okay," Kara said meekly.

As they entered the barn, the horses nickered in their stalls, but otherwise it looked empty.

For a split second, Emily thought it had all been a bad dream.

"How does this taste?" Ozzie's voice wafted across the barn.

Yuck! PhooeyPhooie!

Inside the feed room, a gaggle of unicorns huddled around a big bucket overflowing with a white, bubbly, pudding-like concoction.

The ferret held a large ladle, offering a dripping sample to Clio and Spruce.

"Emily!!"

All the unicorns gathered around the mages.

Dreamer sniffed the bucket and shook his snout.

"No luck making unicorn food?" Adriane asked, trying not to laugh.

"I'd rather eat a stinkberry!" Riannan complained.

"Well, I think it's delicious." Ozzie tasted a mouthful—and gagged.

Emily took a quick survey. "Ozzie, are all the unicorns here?"

Ozzie looked around. "Front and center," he ordered, pushing Violet and Snowflake to the center of the barn. "Roll call. Just like we practiced."

The unicorns scrambled around the ferret as he called out each of their names. "Riannan, Spruce, Violet, Clio . . ."

As each one answered "Here," the ferret nodded his satisfaction.

"Daphne, Kalinda, Ruby, Snowflake, Lysander, Phoebe, Boodle, Harvard, Mailai, Beowulf, Dulcinea, Barnabus, Pierre, Sibby, Quincy, Cromwell, Elvis, Windmill, Zoey, Riccardo, Celia, Electra—"

There was no answer from Electra.

"Where's Electra?" asked Adriane.

"Hey, where are Dante and Ralfie?" Spruce asked.

"And Pollo and Calliope?" Violet looked around.

"Well, that's only five missing," Ozzie said, shrugging.

"Where's Lyra?" Kara demanded, closing her eyes to contact her friend.

"Everyone *stay* here," Emily told the unicorns. "We'll find the others."

The three mages and Dreamer ran to the barn door—and right into a startled Sierra.

"Sierra!" Emily exclaimed. "What are you doing here?"

"I work here," the brown-haired girl said, trying to peer over the mages' shoulders.

Adriane and Kara shifted to block her view.

The sounds of scuffling and giggling were heard along with a "Gak! and a "GarG!"

"What are *you* doing here?" Sierra wanted to know.

"We got up bright and early to help with the chores," Adriane said quickly.

Sierra gave them a puzzled look as she strolled into the barn. "Well, that's unusual for guests, but thanks."

"Ahh!" Kara screamed as Electra trotted up to the door, right behind Sierra.

The mages scrambled to block Electra from Sierra's view. The unicorn tried to poke her nose between the girls' waists.

The brown-haired girl stared at Kara. "Are you all right?"

"I get, like, totally excited by a good . . . chore," she stammered, looking over her shoulder for the unicorn.

Sierra shook her head as she walked to Apache's stall, Electra trotting right behind her.

Adriane made a grab for the unicorn, but Electra stumbled forward, bumping into Sierra.

"Hi."

Sierra gasped. "Where did this filly come from?"

The girls shuffled, looking at each other.

"Her hide." Sierra bent to examine Electra. "It's practically sparkling! Where did you come from, you sweet thing?"

"Palenmarth, on the north side of the web."

Sierra cocked her head. "Funny, I thought she said something."

"Look, Sierra," Emily began. "Remember I thought an animal was in trouble?"

"This is it?" Sierra raised an eyebrow. "She looks perfectly healthy."

"Yes, well, good thing we found them, er, her," Adriane said.

Sierra furrowed her brow. "She must have wandered away from the Triple A Ranch about ten miles east of here." She reached in her pocket and pulled out a shiny red apple. "Here you go, sweetness."

"Ooh, thank you. I'm very hungry." Electra chomped happily on the apple.

A dozen unicorn heads peered from the stall.

Hey! We want apples too!

"What's going on here?" Sierra asked, turning to the stalls.

The unicorns quickly stumbled backward, squashing another. *"GaH,"* from Ozzie.

"Sierra, wait!" Adriane said. "We can explain."

"We can?" Kara asked.

"How many others are in there?" Sierra asked slowly.

"Oh, just a few," Kara said.

Twenty-four unicorns tumbled out of the stall, flattening the ferret to the floor.

Sierra's mouth opened in shock. "I have to call Uncle Tex right away!"

"No, *wait!*" the mages cried in unison.

"We have to get them back to the Triple A!"

"You can't tell *anyone* about them, Sierra!" Emily blurted out.

"Why?"

"Because . . ." Adriane looked to Emily.

"You know that we're caretakers for all kinds of animals at the Ravenswood Preserve," Emily explained carefully.

112

"You mean like Dreamer?" Sierra asked crossing her arms. The girls exchanged glances. "I know a wolf when I see one," Sierra declared, "but I've never seen a pony like this!"

"Sometimes we deal with, well, unusual breeds," Adriane said.

"We've handled animals like these before, and we want to make sure they get home safely," Emily finished quickly.

Sierra seemed unconvinced.

"You have to trust us on this," Emily pleaded. "Promise you won't tell anyone, it's *really important*."

Sierra considered. She seemed to deliberate for a long time. "Okay. I can close off the barn for the day, but you're going to have to muck the stalls if no one else can come in here."

"Thank you, Sierra," said Emily, relieved.

Sierra nodded. "Meantime, I'll get a barrel of apples in here."

YaY!

Sierra looked at the unicorns and giggled. "I swear they're talking. But that's so silly, isn't it?"

"Hysterical," Kara said.

Sierra shook her head and left the barn.

"Oh, this is just great!" Kara cried. "Now I have to muck!"

"She's cool, Kara," Emily said. "And a little cleaning work won't hurt you."

"Sierra may be cool, but others won't be," Adriane pointed out. "We'd better round up the escapees."

"Lyra's spotted Pollo and Calliope out back by the corrals," Kara reported.

"Okay, Adriane, you take those," Emily said. "Kara, you check the spa."

"Right."

And the rest of you," Emily ordered the unicorns. "Stay *here!*"

❧   ❧   ❧

Emily raced between the cabins, almost missing Ralfie's spotted rump. His head was poking into an open window.

"Emily, there you are!" Veronica's smooth voice rang out. The step-monster.

The healer stopped in her tracks. "Uh, hi."

"I've been looking all over for you." Veronica walked up, Pollo trotting alongside.

"Hi, there."

Emily's eyes went wide.

"Look what I found," Veronica said. "Isn't he just adorable?"

"Has anyone else seen him, I mean, where—what—"

Emily caught Dante trying to push Ralfie in the window.

"I brought him to you right away," Veronica said. "I think he's lost."

Emily smiled, relieved. "Oh, good—I mean, I'll take care of him."

"Say, I'm going to an art gallery in town. Would you like to go with me this afternoon?" Veronica's red lips curved in a hopeful smile.

"Um . . . I'm—" She was about to say busy, but managed a more polite, "I have my friends and everything." Emily caught Ralfie's long legs flailing. "I really have to go now."

"Yes, of course," Veronica said. "You know, Emily, maybe I'm out of line here, but I really hope we can be friends. You're the whole world to David, and I can understand why." She smiled.

"Thank you," Emily mumbled, slightly embarrassed.

"Tell you what, meet us at the barbecue later. It'll be fun."

"Okay," Emily agreed.

"Great. See you then." Veronica sauntered off.

Emily caught Pollo smiling at her. "What?"

"What's a barbecue?"

"It's not for you. Come on, help me get the others."

❷ ❷ ❷

It was late afternoon when the girls finished

cleaning the stalls. When they were sure all the unicorns were accounted for, they put Ozzie in charge and left the barn.

"There you are, girls!" David exclaimed as he and Veronica marched toward the mages. "What have you been up to? You haven't been at any of the activities, Em."

"We were—um . . . ," she stammered.

"They were helping Sierra round up some stray ponies, David," Veronica explained. "You know how good Emily is with animals."

"Yes, she certainly is," David agreed. "Come on, I'm starved. Texas Slim promised the best barbecue this side of Memphis."

The mages followed, the sudden thought of barbecue making their mouths water.

The cookout was behind the ranch near the corrals. A huge barbecue pit sizzled with ribs, burgers, hot dogs, and chicken. Resort guests sat on bales of yellow hay ringing a crackling campfire. Everyone was chowing down and chatting merrily.

Texas Slim carried a few mesquite logs from a nearby woodpile and tossed them in the pit. "Come on, fill up them plates, girls!"

"How's it going?" Sierra stood near a long wooden picnic table laid out with biscuits, iced pitchers of lemonade, beans, salads, and condiments.

Emily filled a plate with salad, beans, and a burger. "Okay. Thanks for covering for us."

"Someone is bound to find them," Sierra noted. "We can't keep them hidden in there."

"Yeah, I know. We'll get them home soon," Emily said as she went to sit next to David and Veronica around the campfire. "I hope," she added quietly.

Sunset streaks of bright orange, soft purple, and glowing pink shone with vivid clarity, set off by the dark blue sky. Stars danced overhead, reminding Emily of the magic web. Unicorns were the only animals that could actually run on the web, keeping magic under control and flowing to the right places. Without them, what would happen to all the magic from Avalon now flowing wild?

"Hey, now! What's a cookout without some stories and singing!" Texas Slim crowed.

Sierra picked up a guitar. "I'll start off with an easy one to get us all in a campfire mood." She adjusted the blue woven shoulder strap before placing her fingers expertly on the frets.

Emily's dad smiled and she grinned back, knowing he was thinking of the fun they'd had playing music together in Colorado—when they'd been a real family.

"She'll be comin' round the mountain when she comes," Sierra sang. Soon, everyone joined in.

Emily noticed David and Veronica holding hands and laughing. To her surprise, she wasn't upset. Her dad seemed genuinely happy. For the first time since she'd arrived, Emily began to relax.

"She'll be comin' round the mountain when she—"

SQUONK!

Emily bolted up, startled.

"Emily, we have a problem." Lyra's voice popped in her head.

"She'll be comin' round the mountain when she—"

TOOOT!

Sierra looked at her guitar strings, puzzled, then continued.

"It wasn't my fault!" Ozzie yelled.

"She'll be coming round the—"

BeeP Beep

"She'll be coming round the—"

floohonk

"She'll be—"

Pffoooping

"round the—"

toOOtle

"when she—"

BwAAP!

What the—! Emily looked around at the chuckling guests. Those sounds weren't just in her head. Everyone heard them!

LAAAA! LAAA!

"Whooo doggies, coyotes must be gettin' hungry out there," Texas Slim said. Something green scuttled behind the guests on the far side of the campfire. What was that!? Something *orange* moving the other way caught Emily's eye.

Holding her jewel, Emily sent a telepathic SOS. *"Adriane!"*

"I'm on it." Adriane dashed after the green thing, Dreamer close on her heels.

Emily wondered why Dreamer wasn't in the barn watching the—*uh oh.*

A glittering silver animal followed the mistwolf.

"Wonderful—Anyone else have a talent they want to share?" Tex called out.

ZZZZAP!

Kara yelped as diamond-white magic sparkled in the night like a miniature fireworks display. When the glittering light faded, her hair was a mass of curling purple ringlets.

"Cool, a magic act!" one of the guests exclaimed amid appreciative applause.

Gulping, Kara bowed. "And now for a disappearing act." She dashed off, shaking her colorful head at Emily.

"Okay, we had a song and a—whatever that was—but now it's time for ghost stories!" Tex announced.

Emily excused herself and ran to the barn. Pulling open the door, she gasped.

The unicorns were huddled in a big mass tootling and hooting up a storm.

"What's going on?" Emily asked.

Something sparkled in the middle of the group.

Emily pushed her way through the unicorns. There in the center stood Dante, Boodle, and Spruce. No longer beige, their coats were sparkling silver, green, and orange. And upon their foreheads, swirling crystal glittered.

Oh no! Their horns had sprouted!

"How cool is this?!" Dante crowed.

The unicorns proudly displayed their new horns.

A hay bale flew across the room. Adriane ducked for cover just in time.

A bright light surrounded Ralfie. When it cleared, his hide was a deep green, with bright brass-colored spots. His new horn shimmered with rainbow magic.

"I'm so handsome!" Ralfie puffed his chest proudly.

A perplexed Domino rose a few inches off the ground.

"Everyone! Stop!" Emily shouted. "Listen to me, do *not* use your magic."

The unicorns all stopped.

"What happened to you?!" she asked, shocked. "You're all silver and orange and green!"

"These are our real colors," Ralfie explained. *"They appear when our horns grow in."*

"I thought unicorns were white," Adriane said.

"How many have you seen?" Ralfie challenged.

"Two," she admitted.

"Well, there you go." Spruce said.

Suddenly bright lights flashed—horns were popping up like popcorn!

"Where's Kara?" Emily was looking about frantically. "Kara?"

"Hey, where's Calliope?" Dante asked. *"And Mailai and Violet? And Electra? And Snowflake?"*

"Roll call—" Ozzie shouted.

"Not now, Ozzie!" Adriane yelled.

Hiding thirty baby unicorns that looked like colts and fillies was one thing. How long would it take for people to notice thirty bright rainbow-colored unicorns with real sparkling crystal horns?

"Come to the cabin!" Kara's voice popped in Emily's mind. *"Hurry! We have an emergency!"*

"Everyone just *stay* here!" Emily shouted, running toward the barn door. "Let's go, Adriane."

Chapter 10

High-pitched squeals split the air like a strangled trombone as Adriane and Emily barreled through the cabin door.

"Kara, are you all right?" Emily called out.

"Hi."

Electra, Daphne, Phoebe, Kalinda, Ruby, Dulcinea, Sibby, Zoey, and Celia were lolling about on the beds, pillows, and rugs, looking dazzling in shades of mint greens, ocean blues, lilac lavenders, and sunset reds. Their crystal horns twinkled with magic.

"Oh!" Emily stared.

"What's the emergency?" Adriane asked.

"We need those extra towels," Kara called from the bathroom.

"I think she means these." Emily lifted the pile of towels set on the dresser and opened the bathroom door—into a storm of bubbles. Violet and Clio were in the tub, splashing about in a bubble bath. Snowflake and Mailai were preening in front of the mirror.

Kara sat on the edge of the tub, comb in her mouth, styling Calliope's mane and tail. The room was littered with plastic bottles of conditioner, shampoo, mousse, and hair gel. A blow dryer hung over the sink. Unicorn hair was piled on the floor.

"Cool, set them down over there." Kara ran the comb through Calliope's mane, carefully trimming the silky hair.

Emily gasped. "Calliope, you're . . ." The unicorn's hide had turned an incredible shade of pastel green, iridescent and absolutely gorgeous.

"Green!" Adriane finished.

"And so beautiful!" Emily added.

Calliope beamed. Her crystal horn swirled from her forehead, pulsing with a bright pistachio light.

"Stay still!" Kara ordered. The blazing star's jeans and tank top were covered in shampoo, bubbles, and brightly colored unicorn hair.

Violet and Clio barreled out of the tub and started primping next to Snowflake and Mailai.

"Your horns!" Emily exclaimed, examining the unicorns' foreheads. "They've all grown! And look at you!"

True to her name, Violet had turned a beautiful shade of lavender, her crystal horn glowing upon her forehead. Snowflake had become a dazzling snow white, Clio an aqua blue, Mailai a sunburst orange. The rest of the female unicorns crowded in the bathroom door, proudly showing their sparkling horns to Emily and Adriane.

"You're all so beautiful!" Emily exclaimed. "But what's all this?" She swept her hand over the mess that started in the bathroom and now spilled all over the cabin.

"They can't show up at the academy without looking their best!" Kara said, smiling.

"*Kara would* never *let us jump across the web all dirty!*" Electra declared.

"First impressions are very important." Kara held Calliope's head to inspect her handiwork.

"*Absotootly!*" Calliope agreed, nodding.

"*Oh Emily, we're so excited!*" Snowflake exclaimed. "*We going to make magic!*"

"*We're really going to run the web!*" Mailai squeaked.

Kara sniffled. "I'm so proud of my little girls, all grown up so fast!"

FloooB!

Clio's horn burst with sapphire light as her magic sent a swarm of bath bubbles all over Kara.

"Well, don't just stand there," Kara said to the other mages. "This is a par-*tay*! We're styling!"

Adriane and Emily couldn't help themselves.

They got into the spirit and joined right in. Each took towels and started drying and brushing the shampooed and conditioned unicorns.

Laughing and giggling, the unicorns and three mages took over the entire cabin. Each unicorn was beautiful, horn blinking like a Christmas light.

Suddenly, Kara put her hand up. "Wait!" Stroking her chin in deep thought, the blazing star surveyed the group. "There's something missing."

"What?" The unicorns checked themselves over.

"I know!" Kara leaped to the dresser and began riffling through her clothes. She pulled out several silk blouses. "These will do." Holding up the scissors, she closed her eyes tight.

Emily and Adriane were shocked.

As they watched, Kara cut up her prized possessions into long strips.

"Now I've seen everything," Adriane said, laughing. "Her jewel has driven her completely over the edge!"

"Didn't hurt a bit," Kara said, tying silk ribbons and bows in the unicorns' hair.

"Oh, my *GawD! Kara!*" Emily howled, rolling on the bed and doubled over in laughter. Violet, Dulcinea, Clio, Electra, and Phoebe fell over the healer, squealing in delight.

A knock at the door brought the group up sharp.

"Who's there?" Emily asked, giggling.

"gAh!"

"Come in, Ozzie," Emily called.

The door burst open—but the ferret was not alone. Fifteen boy unicorns tumbled over him, hooting and hollering.

"*Hey!*" Clio said. "*Girls only!*"

"*Wow, Clio,*" Dante said. "*You look . . . nice!*"

Clio blushed. "*Really?*"

"It was a mutiny!" Ozzie stood up and kicked Ralfie.

"It's okay, Ozzie," Emily said, breaking up in laughter again.

"*Check it out, ladies!*" Ralfie pranced about, proudly displaying his deep green hide with bright brass-colored spots.

"*Ooo, Ralfie!*" Daphne, Zoey, Mailai, and Dulcinea crowded around, admiring his gleaming spots and new, shimmering horn.

"Well, don't you all look just incredible!" Emily said, walking about the room, inspecting the new horns. She caught movement out the window. "Where's Riannan?" she asked, looking about the group.

"*She won't come in,*" Clio huffed.

"*Party pooper!*" Spruce blew a raspberry noise.

"Say, you could use a little trim." Kara ran her hand though Pollo's silvery blue scruffy forelock.

"*I want a mullet!*" Ralfie tooted.

Emily nodded to her friends. "I'll be right back."

"Right this way to Kara's unicorn beauty parlor!" The blazing stylist motioned to the bathroom. Ralfie and Dante took a flying leap right into the tub, splashing water everywhere.

"Boys!" Clio huffed.

Emily walked out into the cool night and breathed in deeply. The air smelled fresh and clean. Stars winked across the sky like diamonds. Luckily their cabin was set apart from the others, so no one could hear the party going on inside.

A unicorn peered around the cabin, head lowered, mane and forelock covering her face.

"Riannan?" Emily called softly. "Don't you want to join us inside? We're having a lot of fun."

The unicorn turned her hornless head away. *"No!"*

"Then is it okay if I sit here for a while?" Emily asked.

"I guess . . ."

Emily sat on the front step. "What's wrong, Riannan?"

"Everything!" The unicorn sobbed, dark eyes glimmering. *"What if my magic isn't good enough?"*

"When you get your horn, I'm sure you'll sound beautiful," Emily reassured her.

"You don't understand!" Riannan swished her

nearly golden tail. *"Everyone thinks I'm going to be the princess!"*

"Princess?"

"One unicorn in each generation is a prince or princess," Riannan explained.

Emily was startled into silence for a moment. She'd never heard of unicorns having princes and princesses. "You don't know if it's you or not?"

"Nobody knows until our horns are tuned." Riannan flopped down next to Emily. *"What if I'm not really special? I'm scared, Emily."*

The healer looked into Riannan's deep liquid eyes. Gently petting the unicorn's neck, she began, "Not long ago, I found myself in a whole new place, with no friends. I was scared. More scared than I've ever been in my whole life."

Riannan regarded Emily closely.

The healer smiled, then continued. "Then I met Adriane, and Ozzie, and Dreamer, and Lyra, and Kara. Through their friendship, I found strength I never thought I had. I love them so much, there's nothing I wouldn't do for them."

Riannan leaned closer to Emily.

"And you know what I'm scared of most?"

"What?"

"I'm scared I'll let them down," Emily's voice was almost a whisper.

Riannan hung her head.

Emily gently raised the unicorn's chin. "But I know they also love me, no matter what I do or what mistakes I make. So I just keep trying to be the best healer I can be.

"It's okay to be scared," Emily continued. "But you'll never know how good you are if you don't try."

Riannan nodded and pawed the ground.

"Princess or not, it doesn't matter." Emily hugged the unicorn. "We all love you just for who you are."

Riannan thought for a moment, then stood and faced the cabin.

"I won't let you down, Emily," Riannan said softly.

Emily smiled. "Now, come on. Let's get inside before Kara shampoos the entire ranch."

Opening the door, they faced a tooting, bleating, cacophonous mess.

"Watch this!" Spruce yelled. *"BeeHoobWaaHH!"*

Pillows flew across the cabin, raining feathers everywhere.

Laa LAAA! Others joined in. *SqEEONK! BleeeaH!*

"That sounds awful!" Riannan shouted.

Everyone stopped and stared at the unicorn.

"If we're going to tune our horns, we have to work together," she said.

Emily walked between the unicorns. "Rian-nan's right." She held up her rainbow gem. "Girls?" She nodded toward Adriane and Kara.

The mages each held up their jewels. Her wolf stone glowed bright as she hit the note.

"Nice, Adriane," Emily turned to the unicorns. "Now you try."

TOOOOT! BeeeBOP! DOoWaaa!

Magic shimmered and flowed up and down the unicorns' horns.

"Very good!" Emily praised them. "But technique is only one part of playing music. You have to feel the music from here." She touched Rian-nan's chest, over the unicorn's heart.

"What you guys need is your own song," Kara suggested. "One you can all sing together to focus your magic."

"Hey, yeah!" Spruce blared a line of bouncing bass notes.

Dante and Clio added a flurry of syncopated toots.

Adriane pounded out the rhythm on Kara's suitcases as she sang the first verse.

> *"You're the rhythm that rocks*
> *To the beat that never stops*
> *Be the tick, be the tock*
> *Be the rain as it drops."*

The unicorns cheered as Kara took the next verse.

"You're the melody that soars
Fairy's wing, ocean's roar
Sing it low, sing it high
Let's go dancing on the sky."

Emily stepped in and sang the third verse.

"You're the harmony that shimmers
Like a star, be the glimmer
As the sun gives moon light
Lift the song into flight."

The unicorns all tooted and hooted, Emily conducting as everyone sang together.

"When rhythm, melody, and harmony meet
It's music by heart,
The magic complete."

"Work it, girls," Kara shouted. She raised her arms and shimmied as Clio, Electra, Dulcinea, Snowflake, and Violet danced alongside, shaking tails and manes.

"Okay, now the boys!" Emily called out.

Dante, Ralfie, Pollo, and Spruce slid across the

wooden floor, spinning and jumping, stomping and hooting.

The cabin was filled with the magic of music and laughter.

Notes wavered and settled into perfect harmony. For a split second all of the unicorns' horns lit at once, perfectly in sync, voices all in tune. A rainbow arc of magic swirled above them, twinkling like stardust.

"Bravo!" The mages clapped.

KNOCK! KNOCK! KNOCK!

The cabin door rattled as the magic faded.

"Who could that be?" Adriane asked, getting up to open the door. She looked outside and shrugged.

"Hey! Down here!" a voice called.

Adriane looked at the ground. "Tweek!" The stick figure marched over her hiking boot and into the cabin.

"I can't believe this is happening!" Tweek's arms flailed in despair. "I was out there floating in the astral planes trying to coalesce my earthly elemental particles into material matter—"

"English, Tweek," Kara ordered.

"The web is in worse shape than we'd thought. Someone released all the magic from Avalon! Can you believe it?!" the E.F. wailed. "It's, like, flowing all over the place. Who could have done such a stupid—!?" Tweek looked at the mages. "By the great tree! Don't tell me you did that, too?!!"

"We were *supposed* to release magic," Emily told him.

"Not that much!" Tweek barked. "I just learned nine power crystals were washed away from Avalon when the magic started flowing. And now they're all missing!"

"Well, that doesn't sound good," Adriane said.

"Good? It's positively awful! Those crystals anchor the magic around Avalon. The entire web is going to spin off its axis if they aren't returned."

"Where are they?" Kara asked.

"Nobody knows." Tweek smacked his head so hard, one of his twigs went flying. "These unicorns have to be trained—and fast. They're needed on the web to control all that wild magic until those power crystals can be found."

Emily looked at the other mages, determination flashing in her hazel eyes. "I think the unicorns can open the portal."

Pooobahh! BROONK! Ooahhhh! MeeMEE!

"We have no choice now," Tweek said, shuddering.

"So how does it work?" Kara asked, taking the silver amulet from her pocket.

"This is a fairy map of portals to the Unicorn Academy. The map has been tuned to unlock only with special magic, including your unicorn jewel," Tweek explained. "If the unicorns can open the right portal, it should lead them along the web to the U.A."

"We'll have to go into the desert," Adriane said. "Portals can get pretty big."

"It's still risky. The portals are all flooie," Tweek fretted. "Without an experienced unicorn, traveling the web will be very dangerous."

"We can do it!" Pollo said.

"Yeah, we can open the portal," Dante added.

We sure can! TweeP! The group began tooting, lights flashing in their crystal horns.

"Well, we can't risk keeping them in the barn anymore," Adriane said.

Emily nodded. "They can stay here tonight. First thing in the morning we leave for Dalriada."

Unicorns piled into a heap on the floor, snuggling close together as they settled down for the night.

Violet scrambled under Emily's bunk and curled up happily while Calliope lay on one of Kara's pillows.

Emily huddled deep inside the covers, listening to the soft toots and honks. Ready or not, the mages had to try and get the unicorns home.

"Good night, Clio."

"G'nite, Violet."
"Good night, Dante."
"G'nite, Emily."
"Good night, Snowflake."
"Good night, Calliope."
"G'nite, Fuzzy."
"Good *night*!"

Chapter 11

*L*ight broke into fragments, rippling along tower-ing crystalline walls. Frozen spider webs shiv-ered, draped like delicate glass sculptures.

Emily wandered into an immense chamber of black ice.

She wasn't cold. She didn't feel . . . anything.

Flashes of light silhouetted a large block rising from the center of the chamber. She moved carefully across the smooth floor, trying to see inside the block. But murky smoke ran through its icy surface.

Emily placed her hands on the block.

"She's only a girl!" a surprised voice shattered the silence.

"Do not forget these girls are mages." Now a famil-iar voice floated across the chamber. "They are smarter than you think."

Emily slowly turned.

Several cloaked figures—creatures—sat upon a raised podium, studying her.

"Who are you?" Emily called out.

"She knows we are watching," the familiar voice hissed.

"It's only a dream," the first voice answered calmly.

Emily spun around and dug her fingers into the murky ice, desperate to see more. Parting the smoky blackness, she glimpsed what lay inside—bodies.

She shut her eyes, seeking the familiar sensations of healing magic from her stone. She tried to feel something, anything—but she couldn't. Her heart was numb.

Light flashed. She moved behind the block to find the source. Wild light played like fire from thirty crystal horns piled high.

Emily stifled a scream. She whipped around to the black coffin. The bodies inside— No!

Emily opened her eyes and winced. She had no sensation in her right arm. Turning to her side, she found herself buried under the warm bodies of Clio and Violet. Gently pushing the unicorns aside with her left hand, she slid her numb arm free, rolled out of bed, slipped into her jeans, and pulled on a sweatshirt.

Squinting in the early morning light, she took in the room. It was jammed with bodies. Panic shot through her as she flashed on her nightmarish image. She let out her breath as she saw the unicorns stir, awakening from their sleep.

"Emily," a voice called softly from outside the cabin.

Adriane heard it too. She jumped from the top bunk, awake and ready in an instant, Dreamer by her side.

"Emily, are you in there? I need to talk to you!" Sierra's voice pleaded from the other side of the cabin door.

"Shhh." Emily held a finger to her lips as she climbed over the pile of groggy unicorns.

"Emily, are you all right?" Ozzie flailed and dug his way out of the pile, shoving Spruce's hoof aside.

"BLLEEEAHHHHH!" The startled unicorn complained.

"Where's the snooze button?" Kara's hand waved in the air and bonked Spruce's nose.

Emily carefully opened the cabin door and slipped outside.

Sierra's sweet face was lined with worry. "The barn is empty!"

"It's okay," Emily reassured her. "They're safe."

"Look, Emily, I know you three are involved in something," Sierra said anxiously. "You have to tell me."

Emily searched Sierra's deep brown eyes. She made a decision. "Okay, but you can never tell anyone about this. I'm trusting you with their lives."

Sierra nodded gravely.

Emily's rainbow gem and the turquoise jewel around Sierra's neck pulsed with a sharp light. "All right." The healer called into the cabin. "Adriane, Kara, I'm bringing Sierra inside."

Sierra's eyes went wide, and her mouth opened in shock as the herd of multicolored unicorns with shimmering crystal horns stared back.

"What . . . I mean, who . . . !" Sierra could barely form words. "What's happened to them?"

"We grew our horns." Snowflake proudly displayed her shimmering horn.

"They're not ponies," Adriane said.

"They're unicorns," Kara explained.

"What?! But that's impossible! Unicorns aren't real." Sierra looked closely at Clio's pistachio horn, pulsing with soft light. "Right?"

"We could use some apples." Pollo yawned and stretched, sending a flurry of magic up and down his crystal horn.

"They're so beautiful!" Sierra trembled as she walked among them, absently reaching in her vest pocket for a few apples.

"Thank you," Electra said, stumbling over Pollo to take one.

"I feel like I'm dreaming." Sierra rubbed her wide brown eyes as the dazzling blue unicorn munched from her hand. "Where did they come from?"

Emily grasped Sierra's arm. "I can explain everything later, but we have to get them out of here right now. Do you want to help?"

"We need to take them to a secluded area," Adriane said. "No one can see them."

"The Arrow Rocks," Sierra suggested, though she still seemed dazed. "It's about three miles south of the ranch."

"Any idea how we can sneak them away?" Adriane asked.

"I'm scheduling the trail rides this morning. I can make sure everyone heads north. The path through the riding arenas will be all clear." Sierra said thoughtfully.

"Sounds good," Adriane approved. "Dreamer and I know the way."

Sierra shook her head in amazement. "I knew Ravenswood was special, but I never realized just *how* special."

"Welcome to the club," Kara said.

❧   ❧   ❧

The unicorns marched single file past the cabins and riding areas. Just as Sierra had promised, no one was around to see the strange herd as they left the ranch grounds, crossed the dirt road, and made for the desert.

Adriane took the lead as Dreamer scouted the perimeter, keeping a nose out for trouble. Kara walked alongside the group, while Emily took position in the rear. Ozzie and Tweek, riding Ralfie, scanned the desert. Lyra, her elegant magical wings spread wide, circled overhead, watching from the skies.

"You think we'll like school?" Calliope asked, sticking out her tongue.

"Of course you will," Kara answered. "I love school. You get to hang with all your friends and look cool."

"And you can even learn things, too, Kara," Emily pointed out.

"Oh yeah, that," Kara conceded.

"You're going to be the best class the academy ever had!" Emily smiled.

The unicorns proudly puffed their chests and marched faster.

Emily's smile faded as she looked around nervously. The vast desert stretched in front of them, empty and quiet. It felt so open, vulnerable to attack from anywhere. But they had the all-clear from Dreamer and Lyra. They could make it. They had to.

"Everyone's looking terrific this morning," Kara said, walking up and down the ranks inspecting the group.

Calliope tooted in agreement, head held high. But no one could deny the cloud of despondency and worry among the group. Last night had been sheer joy; now, the unicorns were scared.

After a while, the group wound down a trail that led past a series of rolling, scrub-covered hills. Up ahead, a cluster of tall, red rocks stood in a giant circle.

"There it is," Adriane said. "The Arrow Rocks."

The strange dream nagged at Emily's mind again. She felt the need to hurry, as if they were running out of time.

The ring of rocks pointed to the wide, blue sky like rough fingers, surrounding an area about half the size of a football field.

"Quickly now, I want everyone in the center!" Emily called, the minute they reached the Arrow Rocks.

The mages herded the group through the tall, wide spires.

"Okay," Emily instructed. "Let's get into position."

Inside the circle of rocks, the unicorns made their own ring around the healer.

"Dreamer?" Adriane called out.

"All clear," Dreamer's voice popped into Adriane's head.

"Everything's quiet up here," Lyra reported, gliding overhead.

The warrior nodded to her friends.

"Okay, Kara, open the fairy map," Emily said.

Kara took the silver amulet from her pocket and stood between her friends.

Adriane held up her wolf stone. Emily raised her healing gem. The unicorns prepared to unleash their magic, lights pulsing from their horns.

Kara held her jewel, closed her eyes, and concentrated. "Open sesame!"

"A magical incantation!" Tweek's quartz eyes spun in his twigs. "Fantastic."

A bubble of light blossomed from the center of the amulet, forming an intricate web of lines and lights. Kara stepped back. The fairy map floated before them.

Everyone watched in awe as bright star points glittered and sparkled, reflecting off the crystal horns.

Emily pointed to the brightest light amid an arcing strand of stars. "That one?"

"That's the one that opens to Dalriada," Tweek said, hopping up and down. "Hurry now!"

"Focus on that portal," Emily directed. "Are you ready?"

The unicorns nodded their heads in unison.

"Okay," she raised her arms as Adriane and Kara held up their jewels. Together, they hummed a clear note, jewels pulsing in sync.

BLLeahHHH! DiNG! LaaaaAA!

Horns blinked as notes wavered in and out of tune.

"Eeeek!" Tweek squeaked. "That's awful."

"Easy now." Emily tried to hide her anxiety. "Try again."

Bright magic flashed from their horns. But the notes were all off-key.

"Let it flow naturally," Emily called out, trying to sync the wild lights from the horns to her pulsing healing gem.

The unicorns sang louder, trying to get their music in tune. Magic zipped up and down their horns, sending bursts of fireworks into the air.

Kara grasped her jewel tightly but the fairy map began to dissolve, warping into wavering lines.

"Hold it together, Kara!" Adriane ordered.

"I'm trying!" The blond girl clamped down harder.

The unicorns hooted and honked. Wisps of rainbow magic twinkled above them, shimmering in the wind. Emily fretfully tried to conduct the music but the unicorns seemed to have reached the limits of their untrained magic.

"Ahh!" Kara screamed. The unicorn jewel flared. The fairy map burst apart! Fragments snaked away, and the amulet burst into light and vanished.

"What happened?" Adriane demanded.

"Are you all right?" Emily grabbed Kara's hand, inspecting it for burns.

"I don't know, it just overloaded," Kara said, examining her jewel. "I'm okay."

"Oh no!" Tweek cried. "The amulet is destroyed."

The unicorns went silent, heads bowed sadly.

Then Violet squeaked, *"How are we going to get home?"*

Emily didn't have an answer.

"We'll figure out another way, Emily," Riannan said reassuringly.

Emily tried to smile, but inside, she felt the first tingles of panic crawling in her stomach. This was all her fault. She'd said they could do it, but they just weren't ready. What were they going to do now?

A flash of rainbow lights popped in the air. To the group's shock, a small portal split open in front of them.

"Look!" The E.F. gasped. "They must have opened it after all."

"It's a lot smaller than the Ravenswood portal," Emily noted. Still, she was hopeful.

The shimmering circle stretched to the size of a large door, trails of mist spilling to the desert sand. Inside, a grid of dark purple gleamed amid glowing black lights—this was nothing like the glittering magic web the mages had seen before.

"That doesn't look right. What is *that*?" Kara pointed at dark shapes slithering and skittering inside the portal.

Dreamer ran past the rocks, skidding into Adriane. *"Magic. Bad magic."*

"Everyone, stay together!" Golden wolf fire sprang from Adriane's jewel, spiraling up her arm. "Kara, Emily, by me!"

Emily and Kara assumed positions back-to-back against Adriane. Lyra landed next to Kara, teeth bared.

"BLEEWaaWWW!"

"Shhh, Spruce!" Riannan whispered.

"Something's coming!" Spruce wailed.

"I'm scared! Emily! Don't let them hurt us!" The unicorns trembled, their warbling notes squeaked and peeped.

"Steady," Adriane said, whipping her magic into a lasso, ready to defend her friends.

Without warning, a ball of green light sprang from the portal.

Kara's jewel exploded with bright magic, sending the blazing star rolling backward. She struggled to control the power as Lyra leaped to protect her.

"Kara!" Emily yelled.

In a flash, the light opened. A tangled mass of strands expanded into a giant net.

Adriane tried to deflect it, but the net flew over her head, ensnaring the unicorns.

"AHGHHH! Get it OFF! EmilYY!! HELP!" The unicorns erupted in screams, light bursting from their horns.

Emily ran to the unicorns, clawing at the glowing green net. "Adriane!"

The warrior and mistwolf ripped and tore at the net, but it wouldn't budge.

The unicorns were trapped inside, defenseless.

"Stop using your magic—You'll only make it tighter!" Tweek cried.

"How do we get it off?" Emily shouted to Tweek.

"It's goblin magic. You need the reverse spell—in goblin!"

"Stay calm, we'll get you out!" Emily cried, though panic threatened to overwhelm her.

"Oh me, me, *mee!*" Tweek was on the verge of exploding. "If these unicorns are taken, it will be the end of the web as we know it!"

The portal pulsed before them, billowing like a

balloon. Magic burst forth, spinning violently into a tornado. A wild whirlwind lifted the goblin net, filled with screaming unicorns, into the air.

Adriane flung her whip of golden fire, trying to hook the net. But more tornados of sparkling fire spun from the portal, bouncing off the tall rocks and leaving molten scars. Spinning wildly, the tornados bore down on Emily and Adriane.

"Emily!" Ozzie ran to the healer.

"O' me TwiG!" Tweek shook, twigs flying in all directions as he pushed Ozzie away from a wild magic wind.

Ozzie fell facedown in the warping sand. A whirlwind spiraled right over his upturned rear. *"GARG!!"* When the wild magic spun away, the ferret had a huge beaver tail where his short ferret tail had been a second before.

Oh no! Fuzzy! AHHH!

Adriane shoved Emily behind her as she and Dreamer faced the oncoming tornadoes. The warrior fired a stream of golden magic. Several whirlwinds smashed into the rocks, exploding in colored rain. Emily tried to add fuel to Adriane's fire, but the other tornados were coming too fast. Adriane barreled into Dreamer, knocking the wolf aside as the wild magic closed in. In a blinding flash, the whirlwinds slammed together, trapping Emily and Adriane inside.

"Adriane!" Emily shrieked. She felt twisted and dark power rip deep into her magic.

Through the blinding storm, she saw a dark figure appear in the portal.

In one giant stride, a dark knight stepped out. At least seven feet tall, his midnight black armor swallowed the sunlight and leeched the heat from the air. Red light glowed from the eye slits of his horned helmet. In his right hand he clutched a staff crowned with a glimmering green crystal.

Emily felt the screams of panic from the unicorns.

The knight raised his staff high in the air, green jewel pulsing. Closing his hand into a fist, the knight pulled the net toward him.

"No!" Emily screamed.

AHHH! EmilY!! HELP!

The memory of Lorelei tore through Emily's mind like a bolt of lightning. The unicorn had suffered horribly when her horn had been brutally cut off. *"You have to give up your magic,"* Emily shouted frantically at the baby unicorns. It was their only chance.

AHH! We just got our magic! NOOO!

"Unicorns can give their magic to whomever they wish. You have to give it up, please!" she pleaded with all her heart to the unicorns. *"It's the only way!"*

Amid the terrified unicorns, Emily heard one

high soprano voice soaring above the cries and screams.

"I won't let you down, Emily!" Riannan promised.

The knight stepped into the portal, dragging the unicorns with him.

Chapter 12

In the center of the cyclone, Emily felt herself caught in a whirlwind of spinning lights. Her senses careened, as if the magic was out of her reach.

"Emily!" Adriane shouted, reaching out for her friend. Long dark hair flying, she clasped Emily's hand. The girls held on to each other, trying to steady themselves in the eye of the twister.

"I can't make my jewel work," Adriane screamed, trying as hard as she could to fire her golden magic at the maelstrom. But her wolf stone would not obey. It sputtered out chaotic magical fragments.

"Pack mate!" Dreamer's desperate howl pierced the air.

"Dreamer, stay away!" Adriane called.

Lyra and Kara scrambled outside the whirlwind. The blazing star tried to use unicorn magic from her diamond gem, but she was no match for the terrifying tornado that had trapped her friends.

The wind increased in its strength, squeezing the two mages in its crushing power.

"Your unicorn jewel is only making it worse!" Tweek yelled, hopping up and down.

"Well, do something!" Kara screamed back at him.

"You need to disrupt it with elemental magic!" Tweek shouted, twigs flying.

"Where do we get that?"

"The mistwolf," Tweek cried. "He can change his physical properties."

From inside the tornado, Adriane called to him. "No, Dreamer, it's too dangerous!"

But Dreamer knew what he had to do. His lupine form twisted into mist and shot straight toward the swirling wind. Like a piece of string caught by a spinning top, the mist whipped around, winding tighter and tighter into the wild magic.

"Where is he?" Adriane clutched Emily's hands tighter. "I can't see him!"

Patches of black suddenly appeared hurtling around the cyclone.

"He's trying to take his wolf form inside the wild magic!" Emily cried.

The whirlwind shuddered and sparked.

"He'll be ripped apart!" Adriane screamed.

With a fierce howl, Dreamer's wolf body materialized, flying around the rim of the cyclone in a blur of speed.

Shaking violently, the whirlwind spun off its axis. With a final convulsion, the wind exploded, sending wild magic shooting into the skies. Dreamer was thrown clear, landing in a spray of mist at the base of one of the rock towers.

Adriane and Emily fell to the sands, miraculously unhurt and seemingly unchanged by the wild elemental wind.

"Emily! Adriane!" Kara's worried scream cut through the desert as she ran to her friends. "Are you guys okay?"

"I think so," Emily answered, springing to her feet. She felt surprisingly agile, so perfectly balanced.

"Dreamer!" Adriane made for the injured mistwolf, but stumbled forward. Steadying herself, she ran to her pack mate

"Emily!" Ozzie lumbered over. "Look what happened to me!" The ferret bent over, pointing to his bottom. A wide, flat beaver tail thumped against the sand.

"Oh my—"

"Dreamer!" Adriane's anguished scream tore through Emily's heart.

The mistwolf lay on the ground, gasping for breath. He shimmered in and out of mist.

"He can't return to wolf form!" Adriane yelled frantically. "Come on, Dreamer!"

"Dreamer, you can do it!" Kara cried.

"I'm fading, Adriane," Dreamer rasped, his voice a ghostly echo.

"Emily!" Adriane grabbed the healer's arm, pulling her down close. "Do something!"

Emily knelt by the injured wolf. Trails of mist snaked away like blood spilling across the sands. The healer raised her jewel. She tried to release her magic, but instead of healing power, the gem erupted wildly.

Kara screamed and ducked as a bolt of magic zigzagged like lightning, ripping a smoking trench across the sands.

Ozzie fell back, but his huge tail sprung him forward—headfirst into a gopher hole.

"Wild magic!" Lyra called out, leaping into the skies.

The cat was right. Wild magic had splintered off from the whirlwinds and seeped into low-lying clouds, twisting them into dark shapes. The shapes came to life. Wide wings angled out over giant batlike bodies, as four flying monsters screeched and dove to attack.

Lyra was ready. Snarling, the fierce feline hit the first one head on, ripping it to tatters. But the others swooped down on the mages.

Adriane fired her magic, but wasn't fast enough. Two cloud creatures skimmed overhead as she dove clumsily out of the way, tripping and sprawling to the sands.

"Adriane!" Kara ran to help the warrior.

"I . . . I lost my balance." Adriane spit out sand and pushed herself up. "Something's wrong with my magic!"

"Hold on, Dreamer," Emily said, trying to reach into the mistwolf's pain and fear. But it was as if the connection to her healing magic had been severed. "I can't feel my magic." Emily barely heard her own words.

Shadows fell across the sands as two huge monsters dove from the air.

"Emily!" Ozzie rolled over, bouncing up protectively in front of the girl, but his tail made it impossible for the ferret to keep his balance.

Aiming her wolf stone, Adriane fired. A thin stream of warped blue light shot harmlessly into the air.

Easily dodging the weak magic, the flying

cloud monsters lunged for Emily. But she rolled out of the way, amazed at her agility.

With a ferocious roar, Lyra knocked the bats from the air. One smashed into a rock tower, the other skidded into the sand. The big cat was on the downed monsters in a fury of claws and teeth.

"I don't know what's wrong with my jewel!" Adriane cried, sending another blast of unfocused magic.

Dreamer whined, gasping for breath. *"Wrong magic."*

"Dreamer's right," Emily exclaimed, suddenly realizing what had happened.

"Emily, look out!" Adriane scrambled out of the way as the two remaining bats swooped over her head.

Without thinking, Emily rolled and came up in a kneeling crouch, aiming her rainbow gem. A blast of golden light erupted from her jewel. But it arced wide and missed, ricocheting off the rock towers.

Emily stared at her gem. That wasn't her magic. "Adriane!" she cried. "The whirlwind switched our magic!"

The dark-haired girl clumsily scrambled away from one of the bats. "Then you have to fight!"

Raising her rainbow gem, Emily summoned a wavering bolt of golden magic. The strange new power flooded through her senses. It was wild, raw, filled with a crackling fury that she had never felt before.

The monsters dove again.

Emily struggled to control her jewel's new power, golden magic firing wildly.

"Take a breath, let it out slow, and fire," Adriane advised.

Emily spun around, firing at the oncoming creature. A direct hit exploded the monster into shreds of cloud.

The last bat dove over her head. She rolled out of the way, and fired another bolt of warrior magic, sending the monster banking to the right.

Lyra was right there waiting, ripping it to shreds.

Carefully, Emily pulled the magic back to herself.

"Emily!" Adriane knelt by Dreamer, her face pale with worry. "Save him!"

"Adriane, you have the healing power now," Emily said gently. "It's up to you."

The dark-haired girl nodded, swallowing her tears. Placing her hands uncertainly on Dreamer, her fingers slipped through mist and into the sand below. "I can't do this!" Panicking, she looked to Emily for help

"Reach out with your senses," Emily instructed, kneeling beside her friend. "You are connected to mistwolf magic."

Adriane closed her eyes, concentrating. Her wolf stone glowed faintly blue.

"Reach into the magic and feel it," Emily said urgently.

Bright blue-green coursed through Adriane's wolf stone. Opening herself completely, the warrior reached the fallen mistwolf.

Pack mate in danger. Dreamer's thoughts echoed in her mind.

Dreamer, young and strong, depending on me. Adriane let her own thoughts and fears flow freely, mingling with those of the fallen mistwolf.

Monster will take her away, like wolf mother and wolf father. Dreamer called.

Loneliness clawing at my heart. Adriane cried.

With her I am warrior wolf.

One day will he leave me, too?

Without her, I am lone wolf.

Abandoned again by the one I love the most.

Adriane threw back her head and howled. The desert seemed to fall away, as she let herself be swept into the wolf song, connected to the ancient spirits of the pack.

She ran, strong and free. Her body was a shimmering outline, trailing starfire. The endless forests came into focus around her, timeless and full of life.

Run with us, warrior!

Adriane was surrounded by mistwolves, thousands strong, the thunder of paws pounding the earth.

One wolf broke from the pack to run by her side. The wolf's silver fur rippled over powerful muscles, golden eyes shining bright.

"My heart soars to see you, warrior."

Adriane was filled with joy at the sight of her beloved lost pack mate. Stormbringer.

"Storm, is it really you?"

"Run with me, pack mate."

There was no past, no future. Only the moment as mistwolf and warrior ran the spirit trail together. Adriane felt the ancient mistwolf magic flowing through her.

"Stay focused, warrior. Open yourself to those who love you."

Wolf and warrior arrived at the edge of the forest. Two trails ran in opposite directions, shrouded in mist.

"I want to run with you." Adriane knelt and hugged Storm, tears streaming down her face. For an eternal moment she felt the warmth and strength of her friend, the smell of the forests in her soft fur.

"*Stand strong with your friends. Your destiny still lies ahead of you. I am with you, now and forever.*"

"I love you," Adriane whispered, her hands clasping soft fur.

She opened her eyes, her hands in Dreamer's thick coat. His body was solid and whole, black fur lustrous and shiny. Bright emerald eyes stared back at her, full of love.

"How many times do I have to tell you to listen to me!" she scolded, then smiled, hugging her pack mate close. "Don't you leave me ever again."

Dreamer's emerald eyes danced. "*I am with you, now and forever.*"

"You did it!" Emily embraced both the wolf and the warrior.

"That was incredible!" Kara joined the group hug, Lyra by her side.

"*Gah!*" Ozzie was grabbed and squeezed into the hug, wide tail flapping.

"I must say, you mages certainly make interesting magic." Tweek stood to the side.

"It's called a hug, Tweek," Emily explained. "You should try it."

"I have enough trouble, thank you."

Dreamer stood, proudly stretching his lithe body.

"How do we switch our jewels back?" Emily asked Tweek.

The twig figure looked through images in his gem. "I think you're stuck."

"I never could have healed Dreamer alone," Adriane confessed.

"I could never be a warrior, never like you," the red-haired girl admitted.

"Hey! Being a blazing star isn't exactly a trip to the mall!" Kara huffed.

"Well, actually it is," Tweek said, looking up "mall" in his HORARFF.

"You think its easy being a ferret *and* a beaver?" Ozzie asked, flapping its giant beaver tail.

"A berret," Kara commented.

"It's all my fault," Emily said, frowning. "If I hadn't pushed the unicorns to open the portal, this never would have happened."

"This is bad," Tweek rattled. "We have to report to the Fairimentals somehow and tell them this dark knight captured the unicorns."

"What was that thing?" Ozzie asked Tweek.

"My guess is a hunter, hired to kidnap the unicorns."

"Hired by whom?" Emily asked.

"I don't know," Tweek answered, inspecting Ozzie's new tail. "But the dark knight carries a powerful jewel."

Adriane folded her arms. "We're going to have to work with the magic we've got."

The desert rumbled ominously, shaking the tall rocks.

"What was that?" Kara asked.

On the far side of the rock circle, the air twisted and split apart. A glowing portal opened. Instantly, something hurtled out, crumpling onto the red desert sand.

The goblin net. Inside, the unicorns lay still, as if in a trance. Their once vibrantly colored bodies were pale and washed out. No lights blinked or shone from their horns.

"Oh no!" Emily ran to the unicorns.

Riannan's head fell listlessly against the net, a dulled, lifeless horn protruding from her head. *"Emily,"* she rasped.

"Riannan!" Emily cried. "What's happened?"

"Our magic . . . it's all gone."

Chapter 13

"**H**oly root rot!" Tweek shuddered, threatening to fall apart. "Where's their magic?"

Emily tried to determine if the unicorns were hurt. But her healing gem flared with warrior magic. She swiftly pulled her wrist away.

"My horn," Riannan smiled weakly. *"I got my horn, Emily."*

"Yes," Emily whispered proudly. "You did." But what should have been exquisite crystal was just a dull colorless horn, completely without magic.

"Kara," Calliope whimpered. *"My hair got all messy."*

"Shhh, it's okay." Kara's jewel blazed furiously. "We'll get you out!"

Dreamer growled as the portal pulsed with green light.

"What trick is this?" boomed a voice from inside the swirling portal. Jewel pulsing wildly, the dark knight stepped out.

Lyra and Dreamer leaped in front of the net, blocking the knight from his prey.

The knight turned his horned helmet toward the mages. Red eye-slits pulsed in rhythm with his green jewel.

Scrambling to her feet, Adriane faced the knight.

But Emily pulled her back. "No, Adriane. You can't fight, not now."

The knight raised his staff. A beam of green light began scanning the desert. "Where is the unicorn magic?"

"He doesn't have it!" Emily whispered.

"But if he didn't capture it, then where did it go?" Adriane asked, looking looked around.

Emily and Adriane held their breath as the knight's magic fell over the rainbow gem and the wolf stone. It slowly passed over the unicorns' horns without even a twinkle.

"*Riannan gave her magic away,*" Electra said, shuffling into the cramped net.

"*We did, too,*" Ralfie added.

"*Riannan said it was okay,*" Violet sniffled.

"*I gave it up so the knight could never get it,*" Riannan told Emily.

"Where did it go?" Emily asked.

"*I don't know.*" The unicorn hung her head. "*I couldn't focus it.*"

Dreamer and Lyra growled as the green light moved over them.

Emily felt frantic. She had been entrusted to keep the unicorns safe, and now their magic was missing. She'd failed miserably. "Tweek, how do we get them out?" Emily's voice was tight with panic, realizing the knight could easily pull them away at any moment.

"We need a goblin spellbook. Anyone got one?"

"No!" Ozzie thumped his tail.

"Oh wait, I do." The E.F. held up his HORARFF. "If only we had a jewel that wasn't all flooie so we could focus goblin magic."

"What about this one?" Ozzie held out his ferret stone.

The knight's magic edged toward Kara.

"Hurry!" Adriane urged.

Tweek started riffling through images, letters, and documents. "I have over three hundred different dictionaries in two hundred languages stored in my HORARFF, plus local street map directions," Tweek said proudly.

"*Gah!*" Ozzie sputtered.

Suddenly, the knight's green beam fell over Kara. The jewel upon his staff flared as it scanned her unicorn jewel.

"You think to hide the magic in this jewel," he hissed. "Give it to me!"

166

"Kara's got the unicorn magic!" Emily gasped, realizing where it had gone.

"Makes perfect sense," Tweek said, studying his HORARFF. "Magic attracts magic."

"Stay away from them!" Kara's voice rang out. She stepped toward the edge of the ring with Dreamer and Lyra, drawing the knight away from the net. Gleaming diamond magic blazed in her jewel.

The unicorns mashed together as they scrambled to watch the blazing star. *"Yay, Kara! Go, blazing star!"*

Kara bowed to the cheering unicorns, jewel blazing with power. "I'm back!"

A bolt of green magic shot from the dark knight's jewel.

"Ahhh!" The blazing star screamed as the foul magic encased her. Shimmering in green light, her body twisted into a haggard, green-skinned banshee.

The unicorns gasped. *"Boooo! Hissss!"*

Lyra roared, ready to strike the knight.

"Lyra, stay with me. I need your help," Kara commanded, flicking a tress of greasy hair away with gnarled fingers. Her blue lips scowled. "Nobody messes with my accessories!"

The unicorn jewel blazed, slamming a bolt of diamond-white magic back into the knight. Kara transformed herself into a twinkling pointy-eared sprite with flowing turquoise hair. "That's better."

"Whoohoo, Kara! Yay! Oooo, pretty!"

"Twingo!" Tweek projected a series of symbols and letters in the air. "Ozzie, try this. 'Plithree floob.'"

The ferret held his jewel and called out the translation:. "Feel my beard!"

With a fizzle, Ozzie sprouted a long beard. "What the—?!"

"Fuzzy got fuzzier!" the unicorns shouted. *"Yay! Not yay! Oh, yeah."*

"That's not right," Tweek mused.

"You're telling me, you, you, *you*—!" Ozzie flapped his beaver tail and pulled at his beard.

"Give me the magic!" The dark knight growled, his murky green power smashing into Kara.

She morphed into a black imp with bloodred eyes.

"Black is *so* not my color," the Kara imp said. She turned the magic diamond white and twinkled into a small purple pixie with huge sparkling lavender eyes.

"Okay, okay, try this one." Behind the net, Tweek had projected a new line of symbols. " 'Rathroo migwump.' "

"Fix my shoe," Ozzie called out.

Ozzie's left foot expanded into a huge red shoe "Gah! This is ridiculous! What kind of magic is this?"

"Oops, wrong dictionary. That's pixie magic."

Again, the knight hurled his vile green magic at Kara. The blazing star fought back with a stream of shining white light. The dual forces of magic crashed into one another—slamming back and forth in a magical tug of war. No matter how hard each battled, neither Kara nor the dark knight could hold the advantage over the other. They were at an impasse.

Dreamer and Lyra stood on either side of Kara, guarding her, helping to keep her magic focused.

"You cannot hold out forever," the knight hissed as the blazing star morphed into a massively ugly ogre.

"You're right," Kara's gruesome ogre voice bellowed like thunder. "There is *no* way I'm missing the school dance next week!" The blazing ogre forced a huge wave of magic back at the knight.

"What is this?!" the knight shouted, as a pink halter top now adorned his upper body, matching the bunny slippers on his feet.

"Ozzie, hurry up!" Adriane called out impatiently.

"Okay, try this one," Tweek said, stopping the scrolling symbols at a page of incantations. " 'Ngop maj beembo!' "

"Open the freezer!" Ozzie yelled. A pile of ice cubes dropped on his head.

"Close, but no twig," Tweek fretted. "Focus the magic with your jewel!"

Ozzie concentrated on his stone.

"Bimidee bootilee aoool!" Tweek shouted.

Ozzie held up his jewel. "Release the booods!"

"No, *aoool!*"

"Binds!" The ferret stone blazed with light. "Oh, yeah!" Ozzie quickly spread the golden magic over the net. The green grid that had trapped the unicorns melted away and vanished.

"Fuzzy did it!" Ralfie hooted.

"Way to go, Fuzzy," Adriane said.

The ferret quickly shone the light over his feet and face, removing the giant shoe and beard.

"Quickly now." Emily and Adriane herded the group into a semicircle behind Kara, Lyra, and Dreamer. "Just like we practiced."

"How? We don't even have our magic anymore!" Dante cried.

"And Kara's a—!" Calliope looked at the magical duel. *"What is she?"*

"That was low!" The blazing star's voice bubbled from a mass of slimy yellow tentacles. Still

170

holding the evil knight at bay, her jewel blazed and she became a magnificent fairy princess with shining silver wings. "Much better. Wings never go out of style."

But Emily saw that Kara was starting to lose the tug-of-war. The blond girl couldn't keep this up much longer.

Under the power of the knight's jewel, the blazing star twisted into a goblin with knobbly green feet, then snapped into a whiskery rabbit like brimbee. Finally, she morphed into a scaly, lizardlike skultum, the creature from whom she'd absorbed her shapeshifting powers in the first place.

The Kara skultum snarled, lizard eyes flashing in panic. "I can't change back! Help!"

"Release the magic in the jewel!" The knight jerked his staff backward, extracting a flash of glowing magic from Kara's gem. The magic warped, expanding into the shape of a skultum. Scaly snakeskin shimmered along its reptilian body.

Kara morphed back to her regular self, but her eyes were wide with fear. She held up her jewel— but nothing happened. She couldn't shapeshift!

"This is not unicorn magic!" The knight roared.

The blazing star stared in shock. The knight had taken her shapeshifting magic. The unicorn magic wasn't in her gem after all.

Kara quickly regained her composure. "You really didn't think I'd hide the unicorn magic in here, did you? Oh, like, that is *so* obvious."

Swirling his staff in the air, the knight hurled a trio of magical whirlwinds at the mages.

Adriane, Kara, and Emily all fired their jewels at once. Each mage struck a tornado, forcing the whirlwinds against the rocks. Magic sparked as the rock towers began to quiver and melt.

"BAWeeeeMOWAYYYee!"

A loud, sour note blared across the desert.

Spruce held his horn up and blasted another one.

The other unicorns honked a few feeble notes.

"It's not working!" Violet cried desperately

The knight thrust his staff forward, sending the whirlwinds spinning furiously surrounding the mages and unicorns.

"Hey, why don't you pick on someone your own size!" Tweek's voice rang out loud and clear across the desert.

The Experimental Fairimental stood right behind the dark knight, peering out from the base of a rock tower. "Hey, metal head" The E.F. rattled his twigs at the startled knight. "Perhaps you should try fighting a real Fairimental."

The dark knight glowered. "I will have your power, Fairimental!"

"Stick and stones may break my twigs . . ."

Emily's heart raced, fearing for Tweek. But she knew he was buying her enough time. She turned to the unicorns. "We may not be able to work our magic alone, but we can do this together."

"You cannot defeat me!" the knight shouted at the E.F.

"Well, you're right. I give up."

Where Tweek stood, the air suddenly filled with flying twigs, tiny pebbles, and dusty brown patches of dirt. The valiant E.F. had exploded, scattering over the dry desert floor.

The dark knight laughed.

"Oh no!" Emily cried. "Tweek!"

The knight turned his pulsing red eye-slits toward the mages and unicorns. There was nothing to stop him.

Chapter 14

The dark knight raised his staff, hurling the whirlwinds at the mages.

"Fire together!" Adriane called to Emily and Kara.

Bolts of blue, gold, and white entwined and smashed into the cyclones. The whirlwinds slowed, but kept spinning.

"We don't need our horns to make magic," Riannan called out. The brave unicorn closed her eyes tight and concentrated. A sound, tiny, but sure, came out: *"Poot."*

"What was that?" Dante asked, shocked.

Her horn sparked! I saw it, too. How did she do that?

"Wonderful! That's the spirit, Riannan," Emily encouraged. "Everyone, hurry!"

Thirty young unicorns concentrated now, but all they could manage were tentative poots and hoots.

"Just sing from your heart," Emily instructed.

The horns began to pulse, then squeak and squonk.

"That's it," Adriane called out. Dreamer stood by her side, helping to focus the magic.

The cacophony of honks and tootles blended together, building into a wave of sound.

The knight's jewel flared unevenly as the wobbling whirlwinds began flinging magic everywhere.

Was it working? Suddenly, from high above, a single note hung in the air, strong, confident, and unwavering.

It was Riannan. The unicorn held her horn high. A rainbow of lights shimmered up and down her crystal horn as a surprisingly sweet melody flowed as beautiful as a sunrise.

"Way to go, Riannan!" Ralfie's awed voice came from the middle of the group.

Another note rang out, sweetening the sound of Riannan's melody with a delightful harmony.

Pollo's horn began to glimmer, faintly at first, then shone pure silver.

All at once a flurry of silvery notes soared over the circle, ringing against the wild winds. More notes flowed, blending in perfect rhythm, melody, and harmony. Even the tall rocks vibrated with a pulsing beat.

"Get your dance on!" Kara called out.

Moving to the beat, the unicorns danced,

shuffled, and grooved to their glorious music. Magic glittered up and down the unicorns' horns as lustrous vivid colors returned to their coats. A dazzling bright flash surrounded Riannan. Her coat gleamed like a treasure chest of shining gold and sparkling diamonds.

"Impossible!" the dark knight roared. "They have no magic to make music!"

"We have music by heart!" Riannan sang out, smiling at Emily.

"When rhythm, melody, and harmony meet
It's music by heart
The magic complete."

As the music engulfed her, Emily felt something sweet and familiar. Something she thought she'd lost. Her own healing magic was stirring to life, bright and pure as when she'd first discovered it. Emily sang, healing magic blazing in her gem— stronger than ever.

In a soaring chorus, the unicorns focused magic with the steady pulse of their horns. As the music reached a crescendo, swirls of rainbows cascaded over the circle. The whirlwinds burst apart as the unicorn magic touched them.

"How did they get the magic back?" The dark knight's cry echoed across the desert. "Ak—!"

Something was standing on the knight's head. A pile of twigs and scrub brush leaped from his helmet and landed on the tip of his staff.

"Tweek!" Emily shouted.

The knight frantically tried to shake the E.F. loose. But Tweek held on, prying the jewel free of the staff.

The knight lurched forward, grasping.

"I'm open! Pitch it here!" A "berret," big beaver tail flapping, scurried across the sands.

Tweek threw the gem, sending it flying across the circle. Ozzie swatted it with his wide tail, batting it right through the rainbow of unicorn magic. At the top of the rainbow, the crystal's green glow faded, replaced by brilliant white light.

Adriane leaped into the air, golden wolf fire blazing from her gem. This time, she didn't stumble. Her balance was perfect. Dreamer matched her movements exactly, warrior and mistwolf fighting side by side. Adriane fired her magic straight at the knight.

Flung back by the impact, the knight smashed into a rock tower.

Emily raised her hands high, conducting the unicorn choir. Gold, blue, and diamond-white mage magic mixed with the rainbow magic of the unicorns. Together, mages and unicorns turned the magic on the dark knight.

Surrounded in rainbow magic, the dark knight writhed. A high-pitched scream echoed inside his helmet. But it was not the grating voice of the knight. It came from someone else.

The knight crashed to the ground—his black armor screeched as he sprawled into a motionless heap.

The last strains of lyrical melody echoed over the desert as the unicorns and mages drew their magic back to horns and gems.

"Bravo!" Tweek called, walking from behind a rock pillar.

"Tweek!" Emily exclaimed. "We thought you'd exploded!"

"Naturally," he answered. "That was all part of our plan."

Ozzie strolled up behind him, giving the E.F. a high twig.

"I must say we pulled that off quite well," Tweek told the ferret.

"What'd you guys do?" Adriane asked.

"I made a dummy Tweek," Ozzie explained. "And I used my jewel to make it seem like the fakemental was talking."

The mages were impressed.

"YaY! FuzzY!" The unicorns all cheered.

Ralfie bent and scooped the ferret onto his back, bouncing Fuzzy high in the air.

"*GaG!* Can't you just give me a medal?" the ferret screamed as he somersaulted.

Tweek walked over to the fallen knight.

"*Is it dead?*" Electra asked.

"Quite. Without its jewel, there was nothing to sustain it." Tweek explained.

"Let's see who our mystery guest is." Adriane and Dreamer knelt by the lifeless suit of armor. The warrior carefully raised the faceplate.

"Ahhhh!" the group screamed, all peering into the empty space where a head should have been.

Emily couldn't believe her eyes. "It's empty!"

"It's a golem," Tweek cried.

"Say what?" Kara asked.

"An inanimate object given life and controlled by magic," the E.F. explained.

"Like a puppet." Adriane said.

"Yes," Tweek agreed.

"So someone else was operating it?" Kara asked. "How?"

"With that!" Tweek pointed at the knight's transformed crystal.

It floated in the air now, shining with rainbow prisms.

"Glorious blossom!" Tweek cried. "I'll be promoted to a full mental!"

"What is it?" Emily asked.

"It's a power crystal!" Tweek explained. "One of the nine that were washed away from Avalon."

The unicorns and mages stared at the fantastical gem.

"Wow." Kara walked up to the beautiful power crystal, its rainbow light reflecting in her wide blue eyes. "It's amazing!"

"Everyone in the known web is going to be after this baby, and we've got it!" Tweek said happily, then stopped short.

Suddenly a bolt of lightning split the air. The flash glimmered into a giant circle of light. Behind the mist-shrouded opening, lines of stars arced across infinite strands of web. Two shadowy figures loomed at the portal, ready to emerge.

"Look out!" Adriane shouted, ringing the group in a shield of gleaming wolf light. "I think someone's already found it."

Chapter 15

"Listen to the sound
I'll always be around
You and me
We'll always be
Friends forever."

Music drifted from the swirling portal, a
beautiful song of friendship.

Emily knew that music—she would
never forget it. Just as she hadn't forgotten the elegant creature now coming through the portal,
traveling between worlds. A sleek white unicorn
stepped onto the desert sand, her horn twinkling
with magic.

"Lorelei!" Emily cried, running to embrace her
friend. "I can't believe it's really you!" The healer
buried her face in Lorelei's silky soft mane.

"I've missed you so much, Emily." The unicorn
lowered her beautiful head over the healer's shoulder, her silvery voice chimed in Emily's mind.

The young unicorns rushed forward, horns gleaming, crowding around the mages and the new unicorn. *"Ooo, a unicorn! She's so pretty! How did you find us? Did you come from Dalriada? Did you bring apples?"*

"By the great tree!" rattled another voice from the portal.

Silhouetted against the swirling doorway stood a creature that looked like Tweek, made of branches, thick leaves, and bits of earth.

"Master Gwigg!" Tweek cartwheeled over to the Earth Fairimental. "Thank goodness! Look! We found one of the power crystals!"

"Well done, Tweek," Gwigg's rough voice rustled. "It will be kept safe until the others are secured."

Lorelei turned her sparkling eyes to the herd of baby unicorns. *"Your horns are tuned already!"*

The unicorns' horns glowed as they proudly displayed their brightly colored coats.

"We couldn't have done it without Emily," Riannan said, her golden hide shimmering.

"Lorelei must bring the new class to the Unicorn Academy right away," the Earth Fairimental rumbled. "She's one of the best teachers the U.A. has ever had."

"How cool," Emily said.

"How are things on Aldenmor, Gwigg?" Adriane asked. "We haven't heard from Zach and the mistwolves in weeks."

"Thanks to you three mages, Aldenmor is healing nicely." The Fairimental's voice rattled like pebbles. "The Garden is blooming, and your friends say they miss you all the time."

Adriane smiled widely.

"Dreamer is looking very good indeed," Gwigg added.

"Warrior wolf!" the mistwolf barked, rustling Gwigg's twigs.

Adriane hugged the black wolf. "Emily's magic helped me heal Dreamer."

Emily held her sparkling rainbow gem next to her friend's wolf stone. The two magic jewels flashed with gold and blue light, warrior and healer, forever linked.

"Sharing the magic has made each of you stronger," Gwigg rustled, and then turned to Ozzie. "Sir Ozymandius, you've changed, as well."

"Yes, I'm tuning my jewel." The ferret proudly held up his ferret stone.

"No, I mean that." Gwigg pointed a branch at Ozzie's new giant beaver tail.

"Gah! Can you fix it?"

Gwigg approached the "berret." "I can give you two choices. You may get your original tail back and remain a ferret."

"Or?" Ozzie asked, hopefully.

Gwigg paused, tendrils of magic glowing around him. "Or you can become a beaver."

"*GAH!*" The ferret's eyes bugged out. "I'm already gaining weight! I'll take my cute fuzzy tail, thank you very much!"

A glowing swirl of mossy green magic sparkled from the branch that served as Gwigg's hand and surrounded Ozzie's rear.

"What's going on back there?" the alarmed ferret yelled, whirling around to try and see his behind.

"A very proper ferret tail," Tweek informed him.

Kara clutched her unicorn jewel worriedly. "What about my magic? Is it all gone?"

The mass of shrubbery shook as Gwigg regarded the blond girl. "There is great magic inside you, blazing star. But you must be patient. Tuning it is a lifelong process. With practice, and the help of your friends, you may be able to master the fairy magic inside of you."

Kara didn't look convinced.

"Where were you?" Pollo asked Lorelei.

"We almost got eaten!" Violet added.

"With the web emergency, all the unicorns are busy at their sectors so we sent the centaurs to bring you to

the academy," Lorelei explained. "In case you were attacked, the protection amulet had a fail safe built in to take you to the mages. Once the power crystal of Avalon stabilized the portals in this area, we were able to jump through and track your magic."

"How did you know we still had our magic?" Dante asked Emily.

"The knight couldn't find it because you didn't believe you had it anymore. But the magic was always inside you." The healer smiled at Lorelei. "You just had to believe in yourselves."

"The magic is especially strong with you, Prince Pollo," Lorelei said.

Pollo's forelock poked straight up. "Prince?" On his forehead, a star-shaped blaze shimmered beneath his crystal horn.

Pollo! He's the prince! Way to go, Pollo!

"O' me twig!" Pollo cried.

Riannan held her head high. "Congratulations, Pollo." Looking at her brother's mark, her dark eyes flashed with disappointment. "You'll make a great prince."

"And you will make a great princess, Riannan," Lorelei said.

Everyone stared at Riannan's forehead.

Pollo's eyes opened wide. "Riannan, you've got the royal mark, too!"

"I do?" Riannan exclaimed.

The unicorns gathered around the pair, hooting and honking in surprise.

"Inconceivable!" Tweek cried, twigs dropping to the sand. "I've never heard of a prince *and* a princess!"

"This is a very good sign, indeed," Gwigg rumbled. "Two unicorn leaders will keep the magic twice as strong on the web."

Emily hugged Riannan. "You're going to make a wonderful princess, I just know it."

"I'll always try my best," the princess promised.

"I'm so proud of all of you," Emily told the unicorns.

Tweek's quartz whirled in his twigs. "Well, let's get back to Aldenmor."

"You can't, Tweek," Gwigg said. "You were designed to stay on earth.

The little E.F. shuddered.

"Gwigg, can Tweek come back with us to Ravenswood?" Emily asked.

"You'd have the whole preserve as your home," Adriane added, smiling.

"A little Ravenswood moss would really bring out your quartz," Kara said.

"The mages will face their most difficult challenges in the days to come, Tweek," Gwigg rumbled.

"Well, I—" Tweek twiddled his twigs.

"Someone my own size for a change." Ozzie wiggled his tail. "Join the team, Twighead."

Tweek nodded. "Very well."

Ozzie threw a paw around the E.F.'s shoulders. "Great! What do you eat, anyway?"

"Eat?" Tweek asked. "Why, nothing."

"Perfect." The ferret beamed. "That's more for me!"

Gwigg rustled as he approached the mages. "The unicorns will do all they can to stabilize flowing magic. But we need you to find all the missing power crystals."

"The web is in great danger until all nine crystals are returned to Avalon." Lorelei said.

"Do you know where they are?" Emily asked.

"We have reason to believe that one is in the Fairy Realms," the Fairimental said. "They will be attracted to great magical power."

The power crystal and it floated into one of Gwigg's twigs.

"This one ended up in the fairy Otherworlds. A group of fairy creatures used it to control the golem—the dark knight who tried to kidnap the unicorns. They will try to find the others."

The mages exchanged worried glances.

"There is much to do." Gwigg whirled toward the portal. "Stand ready, mages!"

"I'm going to miss you guys." Emily moved between the unicorns, hugging each one.

"You'll always be our favorite teacher." Violet nuzzled Emily with her lavender nose.

"Come see us for our graduation concert!" Spruce bleated.

Kara sniffled, arranging Calliope's pale green forelock. "Remember, check your mane and tail after every class and you'll look perfect all day long."

"One day we will ride the web together!" Calliope exclaimed proudly.

"You know it!" Kara broke out crying.

"Oh no, Kara, now you're going to make *me* cry," Emily hugged Riannan and Pollo.

Ahhhh! Bweeeee! SnnIFFle!

Adriane hugged as many unicorns as she could grab while Dreamer and Lyra nuzzled the others.

Ralfie and Dante shuffled over to Ozzie.

"We're going to miss you most of all," Ralfie said.

The baby unicorns swarmed around Ozzie, nudging him with their brightly colored muzzles.

"All right, all right, now get going," the ferret said, waving his paws toward the portal. "Beat it, you pests."

Bye, Fuzzy. We love you!

Lorelei herded the baby unicorns toward the portal. One by one, they jumped through. Lorelei looked back at Emily before following them in. *"Until we meet again, Emily."*

Gwigg whirled in after the unicorns. "The magic is with you, now and forever."

The mages waved until the last of the group vanished. The portal swirled closed and winked out.

Emily spotted Ozzie standing to the side. The ferret's back was turned, heaving in deep breaths.

"Ozzie," she said, gently petting his back. "Are you crying?"

"No way!" The ferret sniffled.

"We're all going to miss them," Emily said, lifting the sobbing ferret into her arms and hugging him tightly.

🌀 🌀 🌀

Emily patted Domino's neck as she and the twelve other riders executed their final moves in the Happy Trails horse show. Lining up in the center of the riding arena, the riders tapped their ponies' necks. In one fluid movement, all the brightly splotched ponies dipped their heads to the ground in a deep bow.

Sierra rode Apache to the front of the group and he reared on his hind legs, whinnying happily.

"Good job, Domino!" Emily petted the black and white pony's sleek neck.

Domino nickered, pleased with her perfor-
mance.

Applause and cheers broke out from the crowd
in wooden bleachers set up outside the arena.
Emily smiled as she saw her dad and stepmom
waving to her and cheering. David's arm was
around Dreamer, ruffling the wolf's fur. The mistwolf howled his approval, white star on his chest
gleaming in the sun. Ozzie sat next to Veronica,
happily munching a corn dog.

It was still weird to see her dad with Veronica.
Emily had been so afraid that her dad's new wife
would take him away from her, but now she knew
nothing was further from the truth. Like her
magic, the bond she shared with her dad was
something that would last forever. Nothing in the
world could ever change that.

"Whoo! How about we go for another ride?"
Adriane said, scratching her pony, Taco, behind
his ear. He was nearly all white, with a few black
spots and a flowing black and white tail.

"My last day is going to be spent buried in mud
to get all this dirt out from under my nails," Kara
advised her friends. She smoothed her golden and
white pony's blond mane and adjusted her cowboy
hat.

The show over, the riders followed Sierra outside the corral.

"You guys did great!" Sierra told them, taking the reins as the mages dismounted. "I'm so glad we could spend some time together!"

"Thanks again for helping," Emily smiled. "We couldn't have gotten the unicorns home safely without you."

Sierra shook her head. "Don't forget. You guys better keep me filled in on everything going on at Ravenswood!"

Kara looked intently at Sierra's turquoise necklace. It almost seemed to be glowing. "Your jewel is looking more *magical* all the time!"

Sierra glanced at her gem, then whispered. "Ever since the unicorns came, I've been feeling much more in tune with my jewel."

The three mages traded glances, eyebrows raised.

"Promise to e-mail us and keep us up to date on your jewel," Emily said.

"And any other magically interesting news," Adriane added.

"I will," Sierra promised, leading the horses back into the barn. "I'll see you guys at the farewell dinner tonight." The brown-haired teen paused, smiling. "Unless a herd of dragons shows up."

"Don't worry, dragons travel alone," Adriane said.

"Well, the big ones do," Kara argued. "But

the smaller ones like the dragonflies travel in packs."

"True," Adriane agreed. "Then there's the wyverns, they mate for life."

Sierra's brown eyes widened in astonishment.

"We'll be there, Sierra." Emily promised.

The mages walked over to David, Veronica, and Dreamer.

"That was wonderful, girls!" David praised them, leaping down and hugging Emily.

"Emily, you were terrific," Veronica said, an overstuffed ferret lying facedown over her shoulder.

Emily pushed her red curls from her eyes and smiled shyly at her stepmom. "Thanks."

"Hey, Veronica's got a great idea," David said enthusiastically. "A trip to the Living Desert Zoo State Park! How 'bout it?"

"David," Veronica stopped him. "Only if the girls want to go . . ." she looked expectantly at Emily.

"We'd love to," Emily said.

Veronica's dark eyes sparkled. "They have all kinds of rare desert plants and animals," she explained excitedly.

"Snakes and spiders!" David added with a wink.

"Cool!" Emily said.

"Rad!" Adriane's eyes shone.

"Ewww!" Kara frowned.

David put his arm around Emily's shoulders. "You're so lucky, Emily, to have such good friends."

"Yeah, I know," Emily agreed, relaxing into his embrace. "Daddy, I'm really happy for you."

"Thank you, sweetheart."

Emily smiled. Funny, she thought. Life was like an unending circle of discovery. Questions were answered only to have new ones appear. Mysteries were revealed only to bring new challenges.

How were they supposed to return nine power crystals to Avalon when the Fairimentals didn't even know where eight of them were? How could three Level One mages, well, four with Ozzie, master their magic enough to save the magic of Avalon itself?

Looking at her friends, her family, there was one thing she knew for sure. The magic blazed inside of her stronger than ever. And, like her warrior best friend, she would always fight for what she believed in.

"You know, the Living Desert Zoo has a whole collection of unique species," Veronica said, patting Ozzie's back as he lay over her shoulder.

"UrrrrP!"

David nodded. "I bet you'll find animals unlike anything you girls have seen before."

Emily, Kara and Adriane exchanged looks, their magic gems sparkling brightly in the warm desert sun.

Emily smiled at her dad and stepmom. "You might be surprised."

Epilogue

The Dark Sorceress stood before the fairy creatures gathered in the chamber of black ice. She met the group's malevolent stares with her own icy glare.

"I told you they were clever," she said, her voice echoing along the glistening walls.

"Too clever for you, obviously," one of the fairy creatures accused. A finely wrought cloak covered her face, but inside the dark hood the pixilated eyes of an insect flickered gold and green.

"Your plans are notorious for not succeeding," another creature hissed, oily wings draped behind its wide back. "The power crystal is gone."

Trembling with rage, the Dark Sorceress dug her silver talons into the pale flesh of her palms. Much as she hated it, she needed these creatures. None of them alone had the power to escape the Otherworlds. "The power crystal is right where we want it," she explained in a steady voice.

"How so?" the foul winged creature demanded.

"It is being held in the heart of the Fairimental's magic!"

"Exactly," the sorceress smiled, vampire teeth gleaming. "Can you think of a safer place?"

It had been a bold move, going after the young unicorns. A pity the golem had not captured them. But something much more important had been accomplished.

The cowled creature stood. A swarm of shadowy spiders rippled over her strangely bulky cloak. "We must act now, while the web is in chaos. Once we possess all nine power crystals, we will control the magic of Avalon itself."

Black wings fluttering like a giant cicada, the second creature sneered. "And what about the mages chosen to stand for the Fairimentals? They have constantly proven their ability to be . . . shall we say, lucky."

"Beginner's luck runs out." The sorceress averted her eyes from the foul thing. "I will deal with the three mages," The Dark Sorceress's vow rang across the black ice with deadly certainty.

"No," the cloaked figure corrected, her voice skittering like spiders' feet on ice. "*We* will deal with them. Against all of us, they do not stand a chance."

**Look for the other bestselling Avalon–
Web of Magic titles**
Available now from CDS Books

#1 Circles in the Stream
$4.99
1-59315-003-2

#2 All That Glitters
$4.99
1-59315-004-0

#3 Cry of the Wolf
$4.99
1-59315-005-9

#4 Secret of the Unicorn
$4.99
1-59315-006-7

#5 Spellsinger
$4.99
1-59315-007-5

#6 Trial by Fire
$4.99
1-59315-008-3

KIND News Online

Be a kid in Nature's Defense!

Visit KIND News Online at

www.kindnews.org

The website for kids who care about people, animals, and the earth.

**Experience even more of the magic:
Become an Avalon Clubhouse member!**

To find out more, visit

www.AvalonClubhouse.com

or write:

Avalon Clubhouse, P.O. Box 568, Lowell, MA 01853

(Check with your parent or guardian before visiting any website!)